Garth Jennings has directed many music videos
and commercials. His work includes videos for Blur,
Radiohead, Beck, Fatboy Slim and Vampire Weekend.

He is the director of three feature films: *The
Hitchhiker's Guide to the Galaxy* (2005); *Son of Rambow*
(2007), for which he also wrote the screenplay; and
Golden Globe-nominated *Sing* (2016), a feature-length
animated film with an all-star cast, from the studio that
created *Despicable Me*. He has also written *The Wildest
Cowboy*, a picture book, for Macmillan Children's Books.

GARTH JENNINGS

THE CURSE OF THE DEADLY

MACMILLAN CHILDREN'S BOOKS

Published 2020 by Macmillan Children's Books
an imprint of Pan Macmillan
The Smithson, 6 Briset Street, London EC1M 5NR
Associated companies throughout the world
www.panmacmillan.com

ISBN 978-1-5098-9935-7

1 3 5 7 9 8 6 4 2

A CIP catalogue record for this book is available from
the British Library.

Printed and bound by CPI Group (UK) Ltd, Croydon CR0 4YY

For Caspar

THE END

Nelson Green and his seven invisible monsters have been through a lot together. They have travelled halfway around the world and rescued Nelson's sister from a water monster living in the jungle. They have faced and fought a gang of jelly freaks, teleported by eating an exploding stone, ridden a herd of hypnotized cows, leaped into canyons, flown over oceans, driven illegally and parked very badly, they've been shot out of the sky, raised the soul of a dead buffoon, cheated at rugby, brought Professor Doody and Nelson's Uncle Pogo back from death's door and defeated a truly terrible monster with the help of a cuddly toy rhino and a volcano. But Nelson's greatest challenge lies ahead: he must now decide how this story will end. Will he be able to continue living together with the seven monsters extracted from his soul, or will he have to bring their friendship to a close? He had better work it out soon, for somewhere out there, a mysterious man is plotting to destroy Nelson's life.

It is time to begin the beginning of the end . . .

A BRUSH WITH DEATH

Saturday evening. Dinner-time.

'Well, what would you like to hear first: the good news or the bad news?' Uncle Pogo had laid his knife and fork together on his empty dinner plate. He was nervous. He had finished his food way before anyone else and was now fidgeting in his seat. It was Celeste who answered on behalf of everyone at the table.

'The bad news, obviously. I mean, no one asks to hear the good news first, do they?'

'No. No, I suppose they don't,' said Uncle Pogo, pressing a napkin against his forehead and taking a deep breath that he then released as a dry whistle. 'Right. Here goes. The bad news. Doody and I, we've decided . . . we're not going to be working on the TV show together any more.' Pogo glanced at Doody, who gave him a reassuring smile.

'What?' exclaimed Nelson, Celeste and their parents all at once.

'*Why?*' said Celeste, which made Uncle Pogo push back his seat and look up to the ceiling as if the answer were written there.

'The show's a hit, isn't it?' said Nelson's father, Stephen.

'It is, it is,' agreed Pogo, nodding and smiling.

'Have you two had a fight or something?' said Nelson's mum.

'Nah, Tamsin, we ain't had a fight,' said Doody with a chuckle. He was about to eat another chunk of garlic bread but decided instead to lay his hand on Uncle Pogo's wrist in a show of support. 'Me and Pogo felt like it would put too much pressure on us in the future if we're together at work and at home.' He turned to smile at Pogo.

There was silence for a moment, and then Nelson's mother gasped.

'Oh, you're kidding me,' she whispered, as if she dared not believe what she was thinking.

'What?' said Nelson. 'I don't get it.'

Uncle Pogo shook his head and smiled nervously. 'It's not a joke, Tamsin.'

Celeste put her hand to her mouth.

'Really? You and Doody?' she said, her eyes wide.

'Yep. That's the good news,' said Pogo.

'Ha ha! I don't believe it!' roared Nelson's father as he slapped the table. 'I don't flippin' believe it!'

'What?' repeated Nelson. 'I don't get it. What's going on?'

'Well, see, that's the good news, mate,' said Doody, turning to Nelson. 'Me and your uncle have decided to live together. And on top of that we're gonna get married.'

The scream of delight from Nelson's mother was so high-pitched that for the first time in three and a half years, Minty – the world's laziest dog – leaped up from the kitchen floor and began barking like crazy.

'Married?' said Nelson, who was clearly behind everyone else in understanding what was going on.

'Yeah, I'm gonna marry this fella – you'll have two uncles now!' said Doody, and he laughed at the sight of everyone but Nelson losing their minds with happiness.

'Champagne!' cried Nelson's father as he jumped from his seat.

'We haven't got any!' cried Nelson's mother.

'Oh. What about that fizzy wine the Clarks brought with them last time?'

Nelson's mother pulled a face.

'Married?' repeated Nelson, but no one heard him over Minty's incessant barking.

'Quiet, Minty! Shush! Stop it!' snapped Nelson's mother.

'Wait! Can I be a bridesmaid?' said Celeste.

'Actually, we were going to ask if you would,' said Uncle Pogo. He laughed, clearly relieved to have dished out the big news.

'I knew it! Didn't I say they might get married?' Nelson's mother had grabbed Doody and pulled close enough to kiss him.

'No! You've never said that once,' said Nelson's father, but before she could protest – *Pop!* The cork shot out of the bottle of fizzy wine he was holding, bounced off the ceiling and hit Minty on the nose.

Bark, bark, bark, bark! Bark!

'Minty! Minty, stop! You're gonna give yourself a heart attack!' said Nelson's father as he rushed to pour the wine into the glasses on the table.

It's been said that a brush with death can sometimes make a person feel more alive. A mere swipe of death's cold cloak and immediately your senses feel sharp and powerful, allowing you to experience the true value of things you might once have taken for granted. From the stupidly juicy pear you ate yesterday to the friend who has always been there for you, things that seemed ordinary or humdrum suddenly feel like gifts to be cherished.

Doody and Uncle Pogo's decision to marry, and do so quickly, was the result of a run-in with a really horrible monster. Their injuries were terrible and the doctors had not expected either of them to live, but then a miracle happened: their broken bones began to mend very quickly indeed. The breaks fused in the same time it takes a spider to spin a web, and the two men left the hospital only a few days after the accident, the doctors staring after them opened-mouthed with disbelief.

Flushed with relief at finding themselves alive and well, the two men realized that something amazing had been hiding right under their noses all this time. They were in

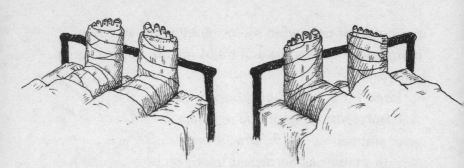

love. They were the most alive, the most lovely and the silliest version of themselves when they were together, and they wanted to celebrate it right now. To sing it from the rooftops! And what better way to celebrate love than by declaring it in front of everyone you know and dancing the night away at the mother of all wedding parties?

(You may have noticed I used the word 'miracle' earlier to describe their healing process. It was in fact a magical medicine administered secretly by Nelson and his seven monsters, but neither Pogo nor Doody knew about this.)

'Oh my gosh. You two are gonna have *the* best wedding ever,' said Celeste, and Doody laughed.

'Mate,' said Doody, grabbing Celeste's hand to squeeze it. 'It's gonna be *legendary*.'

'When, when, when?' said Nelson's mother while clapping her hands.

'Two weeks from Saturday,' answered Uncle Pogo with a slight wince.

'*Two weeks?*' said Nelson's parents in perfect unison.

'We just thought, what's the point in waiting around?' said Doody. 'Besides, they had a last-minute cancellation at the wedding venue so we're getting a good discount.'

Celeste squealed with delight. Minty continued to bark furiously. Nelson's mother turned up the radio that was halfway through playing 'Sweet Caroline' by Neil Diamond, and though this joyful song was very old, it seemed to have been written for precisely this occasion.

'Wow,' said Nelson. He had finally registered what was going on. His uncle and Doody were going to be married. If you had told Nelson this was going to happen before tonight he would never have believed it, but sitting here and seeing how happy the two of them were, it suddenly made all the sense in the world.

And in a bicycle workshop not too far from this happy scene, seven monsters felt what Nelson was feeling and they all cheered for Doody and Pogo.

THE BOUNCING BOY

Stan, Miser, Spike, Nosh, Puff, Hoot and Crush loved the bicycle workshop that was their new home. Not only was it a reassuringly short distance from Nelson's home, it was also private, which made for a much more relaxing

residence compared to Nelson's back garden, where there was a constant threat of being discovered. It certainly beat their other home, which had been with the animals in London Zoo. For the first time since they had been brought into existence, Nelson's monsters felt a sense of peace. Ivan had played a large part in creating this haven for them. Not only was he a tolerant soul who enjoyed their antics and taught them sign language, but Ivan was also Celeste's boyfriend – and Celeste was Nelson's sister – and these deep connections to Nelson only made the monsters feel more at home.

Nelson shared his monsters' feelings of being settled. Only a few weeks ago, Nelson could never have imagined his life would feel this close to normal again. Here he was, washing up plates in the sink while Celeste cleared the table, and not a single worry on his mind. Everyone else was now in the living room, playing music and exploding with laughter every few seconds. It was such a rude and rowdy kind of laughter that Nelson found himself laughing too.

Looking up from the sink, Nelson noticed a light had switched on in their neighbour's garden. It was always doing this because it was activated by a motion sensor, though tonight it hadn't been triggered by the usual cat or cheeky fox.

'He's out on the trampoline again. Look,' said Nelson, switching off the kitchen lights so that they would both be unseen. Celeste peered over

Nelson's shoulder into their garden.

'Oh, poor George,' she said with a sigh. The boy next door, George, was always spying on Nelson's family, and since his parents had bought him a trampoline, George had used it to get an even better look at what they were up to. For George, there was no video game or TV show as interesting as whatever the Greens were up to. Tonight's rowdy dinner party had clearly made George curious and he was bouncing very high indeed.

'Look at him, bouncing up and down. It's the saddest sight I've ever seen. Why don't you just invite him over once in a while?' said Celeste.

'I tried that, remember?' said Nelson. 'We played Swingball together, and then one day I accidentally smacked him in the face with the ball and he left without saying anything. Never came back.'

George continued to bounce in a regular rhythm, his face always focused on their house, his arms stiff by his side.

'He's just shy, that's all. And so are you most of the time. Give him a second chance. He'll have got over being smacked in the face by now.'

'Oh yeah? Watch this.' Nelson flicked on the kitchen light switch and waved at George.

And with that, George disappeared.

'Oh, that was mean!' said Celeste, shoving Nelson in the shoulder and picking up another glass from the drying rack.

Nelson laughed as if he didn't care, but he did care. George was a boy his own age who wanted to make friends but didn't know how, and Nelson knew exactly what that felt like. Not long ago he had been friendless too. But that was before the monsters appeared.

Pinq! Celeste dried her hands on the back of her jeans and picked up her phone to read the text message.

'*Cactus juice?* Do you know anything about cactus juice?' she asked Nelson.

'Yeah, I've got a bottle of it upstairs. Why?'

'Well, apparently your monsters need it urgently. Like, right now.'

Nelson's parents were too busy partying in the living room with Pogo and Doody to notice how late it was when they agreed to let Nelson and Celeste visit Ivan. Nelson was now sat on the back of Celeste's bicycle, his legs spread out wide to avoid getting his feet caught in the spokes, a water bottle filled with cactus juice in his jacket pocket, as his sister coasted around the narrow lanes of North East London.

'What's so special about this cactus juice then?' she asked as they headed towards Ivan's house.

'It's the stuff we gave to Uncle Pogo and Doody to fix them, remember? It's like a kind of miracle cure.'

'Oh, *that* stuff. But I thought you got it from Spike.'

Nelson's monster Spike, who looked exactly like a walking, talking cactus, was able to produce this magical elixir from his nose. Yes, the idea of drinking something that was extracted from someone's nose is disgusting, but this is a story with monsters, so I'm afraid you'll just have to deal with it.

'We do. Normally Spike can just sneeze it out of his nose so I don't know why they need my supply,' said Nelson.

Celeste stopped at a main crossroads and waited for the lights to change. A filthy little white van rattled to a stop beside them. The idling engine made an awful whining sound as if the poor van were complaining of stomach ache.

'Does the cactus juice mean one of your monsters might be hurt?' Celeste had to speak up to be heard over the noisy van.

'I'd know if any of them were hurt. I'd feel it. So . . . so it must be someone else who needs it.'

The lights turned green and Celeste pushed off. 'Well, it's not Ivan. I think I'd know if he was hurt, too.'

The van rattled past them, belching black smoke from its exhaust. Nelson pressed his face into the back of his sister's coat to keep from breathing in the fumes.

'Yuck!' shouted Celeste, hoping the driver could hear.

By the time Nelson looked up from her coat they were coasting down a cul-de-sac lined with old, white terraced houses. Thanks to the street lights, everything appeared a muddy-orange colour, even the fruit bats.

That's right, I just said 'fruit bats'.

'Waaah!' cried Celeste, and she had every right to yell because there were at least a dozen fruit bats flying towards her at head height. She closed her eyes and stiffened her arms as the bats flew right past them.

'Don't worry, Cel! They're only fruit bats from London Zoo!' Nelson looked over his shoulder as the bats vanished into the darkness above the street lights.

'How do you know?' said Celeste, who had thankfully opened her eyes again by now.

'Cos they came into my bedroom once!'

'You're joking?'

'No! My monsters met the bats when they were living at London Zoo. They worked out they could use the bats' high-frequency signals to communicate over really long distances.'

Celeste was still not used to the strange things Nelson told her, but instead of showing how baffled she was, she made a point of forging ahead as if it were no big deal.

'Oh, you mean like a telephone?'

'Exactly! So they used the bats to talk to me in an emergency!'

'So . . . Who else do your monsters talk to apart from you?'

'Uh . . . I dunno!' Good question, thought Nelson. Who would his monsters have been communicating with this evening?

Whatever the answer was, Nelson was sure it had something to do with their urgent request for a bottle of cactus juice.

Celeste braked, and her bicycle came to a stop outside Ivan's house, though it didn't really look like a house. For generations it had been a workshop for timber merchants until one year the owners got tired of all that sawdust and fancied opening a fish and chip shop by the sea. They sold the place to a young graphic designer and her architect husband. With very little money but plenty of ingenuity and hard work, the couple transformed the inside of the warehouse into a home for themselves and their son, Ivan. Ivan was a tall and soulful seventeen-year-old. Like both his parents, he was deaf, and communicated mainly through sign language and lip-reading. His passion for bicycles, especially building them himself, had led to him taking over the workshop at the end of his garden to start his own build-and-repair business. Unbeknownst to his parents, Ivan's workshop was also being used as a hideout for Nelson's seven monsters, who at this very moment were all wearing gloves and freaking out about the terrible news they had just received from London Zoo.

MONSTERS IN GLOVES

The gloves had been Ivan's idea.

No one but Nelson could see or hear the monsters, but by having them all wear gloves, Ivan could not only see where they were, he could also use sign language to communicate with them. There was a fold-away blackboard for the monsters

to write messages to Ivan, but teaching them all some basic sign language had made things more conversational.

One of Nelson's monsters, Hoot – a large golden bird with a silver beak and a very high opinion of himself – had taken to wearing a top hat in addition to the gloves. Hoot thought it made him look even more handsome than usual, and no amount of mockery from the others could convince him otherwise.

As Nelson and Celeste entered Ivan's workshop, Celeste saw seven pairs of floating gloves (and a top hat) rush towards her little brother. She stepped out of the way and turned to Ivan, who was pumping air into the front wheel of a bicycle.

Guess what? signed Celeste.

What? replied Ivan.

Pogo and Doody are going to get married! signed Celeste. Ivan's eyebrows rose to their highest position as his brain processed this information. Then he grinned and burst into applause.

Nelson crouched so that Crush, the smallest of all his monsters, could leap into his arms and cling to his neck.

'HONK!' said the monster happily.

Being hugged by Crush felt wonderful. Like the deeply satisfying feeling of drinking hot chocolate when you're very cold and tired, Crush sent a smile-inducing glow through Nelson's body and brain. Crush had a delicious smell to him too, like the top of a newborn baby's head, with a dash of caramel and a hint of baking bread.

All of the monsters had a distinctive aroma that only Nelson could smell. Stan, the bright-red and angry one with big horns and even bigger fists, smelt like used fireworks. Puff, the lazy one who resembled a large purple cat, gave off a scent that was a mix of lavender, vanilla and dusty library – unless he farted, and then the smell was so horrendous that even normal people could smell it. Nosh, the pink, glutinous, roly-poly member of the group, gave off the unmistakeable tang of the revolting juice that collects at the bottom of a bin, along with whatever he had just eaten. Hoot, the vain bird in the top hat, gave off a fake peachy smell. It reminded Nelson of the floor-cleaning fluid used to mop the school toilets. Miser, the greedy one shaped like a blue egg, with bulbous roving eyes and rubbery roving tentacles, smelt like the school toilets *before* they used the peach-scented floor cleaner. Finally we come to Spike, the envious cactus lookalike, who smelt faintly of lemons.

Despite their peculiar smells, looks and personalities, and the fact that none of them was as cuddly or affectionate as Crush, Nelson loved all his monsters equally.

'What's going on? Why do you need the cactus juice?' he asked now, holding up the bottle. All of them answered at once and Nelson couldn't understand a word.

'Whoa! Stop! One at a time! Miser, what's going on? I just saw the fruit bats outside.'

Though Miser rarely showed emotion, those bulbous eyes of his lit up at being the one chosen to answer Nelson. He cleared his throat before speaking.

'Master Nelson, thanks to the fruit bats, we have received a message from London Zoo. Tango the gorilla is dying.'

'What do you mean?' As Nelson spoke, Crush closed his eyes and hugged Nelson's neck even tighter.

'According to the bats, she had a fight with the new

male gorilla,' said Miser hesitantly, and Stan, who could not bear it when someone didn't get straight to the point, pushed Miser aside and finished the story.

'The bats said Tango's gonna be dead by morning if we don't 'elp, all right?! So if we wanna save her, we gotta get that cactus juice to London Zoo or Tango's little baby will be left without a mum.'

'HOOOONK!' went Crush.

'Can I ask what's going on yet?' asked Celeste from across the room.

'Uh . . . hang on, Cel,' said Nelson.

'Master Nelson, we needed *your* supply of cactus juice, for once again Spike has been sitting too close to the wood burner and dried out.' Miser pointed to Spike, who was standing at the back of the group looking very sorry for himself. Spike's rubbery green flesh had turned wrinkly and woody in texture. He sneezed and out of his nostrils flew a little cloud of dust rather than the usual magic green elixir.

'Spike! You know this happens if you dry out!' said Nelson.

'I was cold! Anyway, not my fault if I fall asleep by the fire. Someone should've woken me up,' groaned Spike.

'Nah, never *your* fault, is it, Spike?! Naaah! Always someone *else's* fault.' Stan clearly wanted to give Spike a slap, but the angry monster wasn't going anywhere near those cactus needles.

'Stop arguing!' cried Nelson. 'I've got enough juice in

the bottle for Tango. Crush and Puff – you'll ride with me. Miser, Stan – you'll ride with Ivan. Nosh, Hoot – you're going with Celeste.'

'What about me?' protested Spike.

'You're staying here and drinking water until you are bright green again, got it?' Nelson pointed to the basin at the end of the workbench.

'Urgh! So boooring!'

'Don't you moan at me. It's your fault you're like this.' Nelson shuddered. In that moment he had sounded exactly like his mother.

'I take it we're going somewhere, then?' asked Celeste as she fastened the clip of her cycle helmet under her chin.

'We've gotta go and save a gorilla at London Zoo.'

Celeste raised her eyebrows at Ivan, who smiled and shrugged in return, having lip-read Nelson's response. She kissed him on his cheek for being such a patient boyfriend, though she couldn't help but wonder when the novelty of looking after Nelson's monsters would wear off.

THE MIDNIGHT BIKE RIDE

Though Ivan's favourite kind of bicycle was a racing bike as lean and lightweight as a coat hanger, it was customizing bicycles for parents to carry their children to school on that had been his main line of work. It was three of these bicycles that Nelson, Celeste and Ivan were now riding through the backstreets of North London.

The bicycles had electric motors at the back and a bucket-shaped compartment at the front that could seat two large children, or in this case, two monsters. A waterproof dome arched over the front section, and though it wasn't raining, Nelson found his monsters behaved better when they were zipped up – especially Nosh, who was always wanting to eat something he had found in the street. This could be anything from a half-eaten chicken leg to a discarded shoe, so it was better to keep him away from temptation.

Midnight had come and gone but the main streets of North London were still busy with cars, night buses and groups of people enjoying their night out. Nelson took the back roads, which he now knew very well since he had ridden his scooter to the zoo many times before. He'd also flown across London, but flying was no longer an option. In the past, complimenting and flattering Hoot had enabled the great bird to grow large enough to be able to fly all of them anywhere they needed to go, but the other monsters hated having to say such nice things about Hoot and refused to do it any more.

And anyway, these bicycles were fast and a delight to ride, especially with his sister and Ivan riding beside him. Though they were racing to attend an emergency situation, Nelson felt very happy indeed. Here he was with his monsters, on a mission he knew for sure would end in success, thanks to the cactus juice. One sip and that poor gorilla would be well again by the time the sun was up.

'Ding! Ding! Coming through!' Celeste laughed as she overtook Nelson and shot out into a brightly lit car park that led towards a footbridge crossing Regent's Canal. Hoot and Nosh, who were travelling in the front of Celeste's bike, unzipped the cover and started taunting Nelson.

'We da fastest! You da losers!' bellowed Nosh.

'Toodle-pip, slowcoach!' sang Hoot.

The compartment on the front of Nelson's bike unzipped and Puff stuck out his head, surprising Nelson by shouting, 'Go on! Get after them, Nelson!' Puff rarely wanted to do anything quickly. As if that weren't enough encouragement, Crush climbed up on to Nelson's handlebars and began to honk relentlessly.

'HONK! HONK! HONK!'

'All right! All right! I'll catch up!' Nelson laughed. He flicked the electric bike into HIGH POWER mode and . . . *whoosh!* It felt as if a great wind were blowing him over the bridge.

'HONK! HONK! HONK!'

Nelson drew up beside Celeste on the other side of the bridge and the monsters roared insults at each other.

'They're shouting pretty rude stuff at each other right now,' Nelson explained to his sister.

'Really? What are they saying?'

Before Nelson could answer – *whoosh!* – Ivan had shot right past them, Stan leaning out of the front compartment and blowing a raspberry so loud it sounded like a passing motorcycle.

Thanks to their silly race, they had made good time and were now in Regent's Park, where they leaned their bikes against the perimeter fence of the zoo. The clouds hovering above the park glowed with orange city light while below the occasional late-night jogger or groups of unsteady-looking people could be seen passing through the pools of lamplight along the pathways. On the other side of the fence, the zoo was a dark cluster of buildings and Nelson spotted the fruit bats circling above. Bats always give the impression of being in a state of panic when they fly, but tonight they really were in a frenzy.

'Wait here with Ivan, Cel,' he said.

'OK. Are all the monsters going with you too?'

'Yeah. It's better if we're all together. Whenever we split up, things always go wrong.'

'Ready when you are, dear boy!' crowed Hoot, who was now hatless and gloveless, and, like his fellow monsters, completely invisible to anyone but Nelson.

'Right!' said Nelson as he clapped his hands together. 'Stan, help the others over the fence and wait for me by the gorilla house. Hoot, you're gonna fly Nosh on to the roof of the gorilla house.'

'As you wish, but what about you?' asked Hoot.

'I'll be inside Nosh.'

'Yah! Nelly-son hidin' in ma tum-tum!' sang Nosh.

'Nelse? What do you mean, you'll be *inside* Nosh?' said Celeste, who looked appalled at the idea.

'Believe me,' replied Nelson as he began jogging on the spot. 'I'd rather not do this. Seriously, it's the most disgusting thing ever, but there are security cameras all over the zoo and if I'm inside Nosh I'll be invisible to them.'

It was one of the weirdest things Celeste had ever heard her brother say, and it was about to be the weirdest thing she had ever seen.

'Doesn't Nosh burn everything he eats?'

'Yup, that's why we've gotta be really, really quick – so he can spit me out before I get cooked in his stomach.'

Ivan had read Nelson's lips and held up his hand for Nelson to high-five. Unlike Celeste, Ivan had plenty of faith in Nelson and the monsters, and he was excited to see what happened next.

For a few moments, Nelson continued to jog on the spot and take deep breaths as if he were preparing to dive into a pool rather than climb inside a monster.

'Can't you just stay here and let your monsters go into the zoo and do it for you?' asked Celeste.

Nelson shook his head. 'They're a total mess without me.'

Celeste and Ivan could not hear Nelson's monsters roar in protest at what he had just said, even though it was completely true.

'See you in a bit,' said Nelson. To Ivan and Celeste it appeared Nelson was climbing into an invisible box. He paused for a moment, his lower half completely invisible, before taking one last deep breath, holding his nose, crouching, and vanishing out of sight.

Ivan grinned and shook his head in disbelief. *Cool*, he signed, but this only made Celeste feel more concerned for her little brother. Ivan loved the weirdness that came along with the monsters, even if it was a bit dangerous. Celeste gripped the railings and scanned the zoo for signs of Nelson or the monsters.

Hoot flapped his wings and hovered in the air, Nosh took hold of Hoot's dangling right foot, and up and over the fence they flew. Even while squashed inside Nosh's foul belly, sitting in a pink soup of semi-digested gloop, Nelson could hear the wail of a dying gorilla.

OPERATION TANGO

Tango lay on her back, her breathing shallow and fast, her magnificent head rolling from side to side on the wide table. She was in a medical room for treating the larger zoo animals. The floor was tiled white, the walls were lime green, and everything, from the washbasin to the table Tango lay on, was made of metal. So many bright lights blazed from the ceiling that all shadows had been banished. The terrible fight Tango had had with the new male gorilla had been in defence of her baby, Kiki, who remained completely unharmed thanks to her mother's bravery. The  wounds that covered her body might have healed in time, but the injuries inside were beyond repair.

Dr Moyse, the veterinary surgeon, had already prepared the injection that would end Tango's suffering.

She tapped the needle and squirted a little of the liquid into the air to clear it of bubbles. Dr Moyse was in her early fifties and wore blue rubber gloves, yellow rubber boots and bottle-green overalls. She turned to Catherine, the zookeeper, who was wearing the same outfit as Dr Moyse (only messier); Catherine swatted away another tear. Ever since Tango arrived as an infant at London Zoo, Catherine had been her main keeper. She had been there for every significant moment, including Kiki's birth, and Catherine felt as close to the gorilla as if they were family. What a horrible night this was. Catherine knew there was no way to save Tango, that it was unfair to let her suffer a moment longer, and so she nodded for Dr Moyse to proceed.

Dr Moyse held the needle against the shaved patch of fur just above Tango's wrist. Catherine turned away and sobbed as she hugged the baby gorilla even tighter. The needle punctured Tango's skin, but before Dr Moyse could push the fatal medicine out of the syringe and into Tango's bloodstream, she fell to the floor with a great *thwump!*

Catherine turned around and was stunned to find not just the vet lying on the floor, but a cloud of foul-smelling purple smoke swirling around her. She would have cried out, or even run to help Dr Moyse, but a second later, Catherine was lying on the floor too.

Nelson stood beside Tango's head holding the bottle of cactus juice. He pressed a scarf over his nose and mouth to avoid the stinking purple gas while the rest of his body dripped with Nosh's slobber.

'Out you go, you foul purple gas! Aargh! Be gone! Yucky-poo-poo!' Hoot was in charge of fanning the gas back out of the door. It was not a job he cherished. Nosh was still outside and letting off a great blast of flames through the top of his head. He had managed to avoid incinerating Nelson before they touched down, but carrying Nelson in his belly had made him extremely hungry, so he had tucked into a bucket of damp, used straw and was greedily chugging it down. Trust me, you don't want to know why the straw was damp.

Nelson looked down at Tango. To him, gorillas belonged in the same category as mountains, thunderstorms or great waves crashing against the sand: beautiful but scary. Nelson felt both a little frightened and very lucky to be in the presence of such a magnificent creature.

He unscrewed the top of the bottle and tentatively held it over Tango's mouth, but he could feel only the faintest breath against the skin of his hand.

'What are ya waiting for? Give 'er the juice,' whispered Stan.

Nelson nodded.

Stan took hold of Tango's head and lifted it ever so slightly from the table. At the same time, Miser's rubbery arms snaked up over the table and his little hands prised open Tango's lips.

Nelson poured some of the cactus juice into Tango's mouth.

'How much should I give her?' whispered Nelson.

'All of it,' said Stan and Miser in unison. Tango was huge and needed all the help she could get.

As Nelson continued to pour the green juice into Tango's mouth, he felt the soft pressure of Puff circling his legs and ankles, just like a cat in need of cat food.

'Ummm, Nelson?' Puff said. 'That's a . . . a lot of juice. I mean . . . who knows . . . how she'll react after all that, so . . . so I think we, uh . . . we all better get ready to run.' Everyone nodded in agreement as Puff started plodding towards the door.

Glug, glug, glug.

There was a gentle crackling sound, and Nelson looked down to see the patch of shaved fur on Tango's arm growing back. The wounds that covered her body began to shrink and heal, while inside her the more serious injuries were being reversed. Some of the cactus juice dribbled out of the corners of Tango's mouth. When the bottle was empty, Miser closed her mouth and Stan gently laid her head back on the table.

Instantly Tango's eyes flashed open, and she roared – a triumphant and stunningly loud roar that made Nelson's eyes vibrate. He had heard some pretty good roars in his time, but this would take some beating.

'Go! Go! Go!' yelped Nelson as he sped towards the door, and the other monsters followed him at such great speed that they all became stuck in the doorway – a tangle of tentacles, wings and claws all scrabbling to get free.

'Oh! Yes, she's clearly on the mend!' said Hoot.

Nelson pulled the monsters free and quickly herded them through the door one at a time. Looking back into the room, he saw Tango spring up and leap from the table towards Crush, who was at the back of the queue.

'Honk! Honk!' said Crush as he hugged Tango's leg and then ran after Nelson, who closed the door after them.

As Nelson climbed back into Nosh for the return journey, Tango sat on the floor and stroked Catherine's hair.

'That zookeeper and vet are going to have the most amazing shock when they wake up,' said Nelson as he tried to flick Nosh's slobber from his arms. Much to his sister's relief, they were back in the park.

'Are you sure they'll be safe?' said Celeste, fastening the buckle on her bicycle helmet.

Nelson didn't answer right away as the monsters were all talking.

'They'll be fine,' he said eventually. 'Puff says it was a light dose of sleeping gas and they'll be awake soon.'

'Good,' she said as she threw her leg over the bike and settled into the saddle. 'Oh, and I texted Mum. I said we were at Ivan's watching a film and we'd be back as soon as it's over.'

Nelson grinned, and felt the rush of cold night air dry

his teeth. It was a thrill to be part of a gang of secret heroes riding home on bicycles through the city at night. On top of having saved a gorilla, they carried with them the prospect of Pogo and Doody's wedding. Nelson couldn't stop smiling. Even with Hoot flying above them singing the worst version of 'Man! I Feel Like a Woman!' he had heard in his life, it was the best night ever.

IT WAS THE
WORST NIGHT EVER

By the time they had returned to Ivan's house they were exhausted, and their warm beds were calling to them. Spike had clearly followed Nelson's instructions, as his flesh was now plump and green from drinking plenty of water, though he continued to gaze at the log burner, hypnotized by the flames. Nelson yawned, and all seven of his monsters yawned too.

You need a haircut, signed Celeste to Ivan, who had just taken off his cycle helmet.

He looked at his reflection in the window and nodded in agreement.

I'll do it tomorrow after school, signed Celeste, and then turned to Nelson. 'When was the last time I cut your hair?'

'Dunno?' said Nelson with a shrug. He was distracted by the conversation his monsters were having about whether Stan should have the tips of his horns rounded to prevent accidents. 'Shall we go home, Cel?'

'Wait,' said Celeste, and she put her hand on the back of Nelson's neck. 'That's amazing. Your hair. It feels like I just cut it this second but it must be months since I did.

It's not grown even a tiny bit.'

The monsters went from chattering to silence.

'What?' said Nelson. 'Why have you all gone quiet?'

The monsters did not answer. They bowed their heads and avoided looking Nelson in the eye.

'What's wrong, Nelse?' asked Celeste.

'I don't know, but something is, and I'm waiting for them to tell me.'

'Well?' asked Nelson. 'What is it?'

'I'm not tellin' him,' growled Stan.

'Me neither,' said Puff.

'Well, don't look at me,' said Hoot. 'I don't want to be the one to tell Nelson he's cursed.'

'Cursed? What do you mean, cursed?' said Nelson. The monsters all groaned, except for Crush, who honked quietly.

'Nice one, genius,' said Stan to Hoot, who had only just realized his mistake.

'Oh, great!' wailed Spike. 'That's it. The fun's over. Not that I had much fun.'

'What is it?' said Celeste, sensing that the atmosphere had changed.

'Well, might as well get it over with now you've said it, Hoot.' Spike turned to Nelson, took a deep breath, and said, 'You're cursed, Nelson, because . . . because, well, you can never grow up as long as you have us around. As long as you have monsters. That's why your hair's not been growing.'

34

Nelson didn't reply straight away. It was an awful lot to take in at once. Crush let out a little honk of support.

'I can't grow up?' asked Nelson. His monsters nodded solemnly.

'What, so this is it? Seriously, I'm stuck exactly like this forever? I won't get any taller . . . or grow a beard or have a deeper voice or any of that stuff?'

Celeste was startled by hearing this but knew better than to interrupt right now. Instead she squeezed her little brother's shoulders. Ivan sat on a stool beside them, aware that something bad was happening.

'Course ya gonna grow up. It's just that you can't do it with us around. So we 'ave to go,' said Stan, his bottom lip quivering.

'Go?' said Nelson, his voice breaking. 'But I don't want you to go. And why didn't you tell me this before?'

The monsters began to wail and pace the room.

'We knew this day would come; we just wanted to put it off for as long as possible,' said Spike.

''Tis for the best. We *must* leave you,' said Miser.

'He's right, Nelson,' said Puff with a great sigh. 'You can't grow up . . . with a bunch of monsters hanging around you.'

'Yes I can! I don't want to change or grow up anyway. I hate beards! I want to stay like this. Besides, we're connected,' pleaded Nelson. 'So it doesn't matter where you go, we'll always be connected. Right?'

Celeste looked anxiously at Ivan, who held her hand as

35

he watched Nelson's side of the conversation.

'We have to go somewhere that breaks that connection and never come back,' said Spike with a weary shake of his head.

'Go where?'

'We must cease to exist,' whispered Miser.

'You mean you have to die.' Nelson flinched. It was horrible to hear those words come out of his own mouth. The monsters shuddered as if a freezing breeze had swept over them.

Nelson knew very well how hard it was to destroy a monster. It took being consumed by Earth Fire, or in other words a volcano, to do the job properly, and the idea of his monsters leaping to a fiery death made Nelson's face crumple.

Crush squeezed Nelson's leg. Usually he could fill Nelson with warmth and love, but Crush was too sad to summon these feelings now.

Celeste cuddled Nelson too, but it didn't stop the tears spilling down his cheeks.

'No, no, no! Don't worry, Nelly-son,' said Nosh between quiet little sobs of his own. 'We not gonna jump in da volcano or die or nuffin'. We gotta plan!'

'Then what? Where are you gonna go?'

'Nosh is correct. We knew this day would come and planned accordingly. You may recall how we sought to contain Master Buzzard's soul?' said Miser.

Nelson nodded. How could he forget? They had used a

needle from the sin extractor, which had a tiny part of the man's soul on its tip. Then they had contained it within a cuddly toy rhino, which had started to walk and talk and had been very grumpy indeed (just like Buzzard himself).

'Well, we learned something from this experience. The same needles that extracted us from you, when turned upside down, can have the reverse effect. They draw us in.'

Nelson could remember the night they had taken a needle from the sin extractor and how the monsters had been drawn to it – as if they were dust being sucked up by a vacuum cleaner.

'Yeah, but I don't understand.' Nelson shook his head.

'We believe – at least, we sincerely hope – that if a needle were to be inserted safely into your skin, it would draw us all back inside of you,' explained Miser.

'Not so bad, eh? It'll just be like it was before we came along,' said Puff, making an effort to smile.

'But it was rubbish before you came along. I don't want to go back to that. I don't want you to go.'

'You wanna tell me what's going on now, Nelse?' said Celeste, but Nelson couldn't speak. His throat was clenched and tears were streaming down his cheeks.

And as he cried the monsters howled. It was the saddest sound in the universe, though no one in the universe could hear it but Nelson.

FETCH

Nelson was supposed to be watching the 3D printer generate the plastic tree he had designed in his design technology class, but instead he was looking out of the window. The sun was shining on the sports field and the shadow of a fast-moving cloud whipped across it. Life at school was better than it had ever been: he had been enjoying some of the lessons, and the boys he played rugby with didn't hate him any more. None of this concerned Nelson right now, though. All he could think about was the idea of losing his monsters, never seeing them again. Would he just feel sad for the rest of his life?

One thing was for sure: he really had stopped growing. It wasn't just his hair, his whole body had stopped. Even his fingernails hadn't grown back since he had bitten them months ago. He thought really hard about whether he could put up with staying the way he was now forever. How would it feel to watch everyone in his class grow up and leave him behind? To see them all turn into adults and do grown-up things while he remained a child?

'It's done. You can take it out now,' said Katy Newman, one of Nelson's classmates.

'Oh yeah,' said Nelson absent-mindedly, and he opened the cabinet. His boring plastic tree seemed unworthy of the brilliant 3D printer. It was like the best chef in the world saying they will make whatever you want and you asking them in reply for a piece of toast.

'I'm putting on a play at the end of the year. We're going to do *Bugsy Malone*,' said Katy, but Nelson didn't hear a word she said.

The school cafeteria was filled with loud children pushing bad food around plastic plates. Nelson stared at his bowl of rice pudding.

'Nosh would love this,' he thought, stirring the gloopy pudding. If his monsters were successfully returned to his soul, would he feel them there? Would they be like voices inside his head? Might they be able to control him, or even talk to him? He couldn't imagine life without them.

Katy came to sit beside him. She had eaten her lunch and was finishing off her carton of apple juice.

'So do you think your uncle could help us make the splurge guns?'

Katy always did this. She would start a conversation with you as if you had been listening to the thoughts in her head prior to her speaking. It was always confusing and always annoying.

'What?' said Nelson.

'The splurge guns. For my production of *Bugsy*

39

Malone? You will be in it, won't you?'

Nelson let out a long 'Ummmm' in reply.

'I can't promise anything, but let's just say *I* think you'd be perfect for Bugsy.' Katy winked, which only served to confuse Nelson even more. He could remember the film, full of singing kids dressed as gangsters shooting each other with splurge guns, but he was finding it hard to concentrate.

Katy reached the end of her apple juice with a loud *shhhlurp!*

'So do you think your clever inventor uncle—'

'My Uncle Pogo.'

'Yes. Do you think he could help us make the guns that shoot out foam?'

'Uhhh . . .'

Nelson's phone buzzed in his pocket. He quickly pulled it out and rejected the call, checking that none of the teachers had noticed.

'Ooh, we're not supposed to have phones on during school time,' said Katy.

Nelson knew this. He had forgotten to put his in his locker.

'Weird. It was my Uncle Pogo.'

'Oh, it's a sign! It's totally a sign! You have to ask him to do it now! Mmm. Apple juice. Are you going to drink that?' Katy picked up Nelson's carton of apple juice.

'Um. No, that's OK. You can have it,' said Nelson,

though she had already punctured the little foil hole with the straw before he had finished answering.

Ping! A text had arrived from Uncle Pogo.

> Nelse. Swing by after school.
> Love, Pogo.

'It's your uncle, isn't it? What does the message say?' asked Katy eagerly, before popping the straw in her mouth and draining the carton of apple juice.

'Uhh . . . just that I should visit him after school.'

Katy slammed the empty carton on the table and clapped her hands, delighted to see everything going the way she wanted it.

'Splurge guns,' she said, jumping up from her seat and pointing her fingers like pistols at Nelson. 'He *has* to make them for us. Beg him if you must. They are essential for my play.'

And off she went, leaving Nelson feeling like he'd just stepped off a roller coaster.

The school bell rang.

Lunch break was over.

It was time to go back to class.

Nelson scraped the rice pudding into the bin and thought of his monsters. They would probably be sitting in Ivan's workshop feeling the same as him. Gloomy. Confused. Scared.

*

Nelson was right: his monsters were feeling the same as him.

But they were not moping around in Ivan's workshop.

They had just arrived in a busy London street and were about to commit daylight robbery.

BREAK GLASS IN CASE
OF EMERGENCY

Nelson's monsters had become seasoned bus travellers from their time spent commuting between London Zoo and Nelson's house.

To avoid interacting with fellow commuters, they never rode inside, always on the roof. It was fairly easy to jump from the roof of a stationary bus on to the roof of a bus stop, and though the loud *thuds* sometimes startled people standing below, most of the time no one noticed due to their ears being plugged with headphones and their attention drawn to their mobile phones.

'Everybody off!' shouted Stan as the bus came to a stop outside the Museum of London.

'Why do we have to do this now? Can't we just put it off for a bit longer?' groaned Spike.

'Longer we leave it, worse it's gonna be when it comes to saying goodbye to Nelson,' snapped Stan. 'We've 'ad good times, and now our time's up, so let's just get it over with.'

'Awww . . . Being sad make me wanna eat somefing,' said Nosh, grabbing his belly as it rumbled like a little thunderstorm.

'Wait until we have completed the mission,' hissed Miser, who was sliding down the side of the bus stop on to the pavement. 'Once we have the needle you can reward yourself with any snack you choose.'

'Can I have mangoes please? Dem mangoes is my best fav'rite,' said Nosh eagerly. He had only just discovered mangoes a few days before and had nearly exploded with happiness at how delicious they were.

'You can have all the mangoes you want. Now keep up.'

The monsters took care to avoid bumping into the people walking towards the museum, and when they reached the ticket desk, Miser took a complimentary map.

'This way,' said Miser, and off they went, shuffling right past the museum guards.

The delightful murmur of curious visitors, together with the beautifully lit exhibits, captivated the monsters, and for a short while they forgot all about their mission.

'Ooooh,' moaned Nosh, pointing to a large jawbone belonging to a woolly mammoth who had roamed the place where Trafalgar Square now stood.

'Yikes,' said Hoot, as they passed a dramatic painting depicting the Great Fire that consumed almost all of London in 1666.

'Honk!' honked Crush, pointing to a little pair of swimming trunks worn in the 2012 Olympics.

'Keep up,' growled Stan to Puff, who had slowed down and fallen behind. There was something about museums – the low-level lighting and the hum of human chatter – that made Puff feel even more sleepy than usual.

'There it is,' said Miser, pointing to the other side of the room, and the monsters bumbled to a stop. They were looking at a great display of all the inventions belonging to Sir Christopher Wren that Doody and Pogo had discovered at St Paul's Cathedral and then tested together on their TV show. There were even two life-sized cardboard cut-outs of Pogo and Doody standing at the side of the exhibit. Among the exhibits was the sin extractor, and though visitors were peering closely at this device, it was contained within a clear plastic box to protect people from its rough metal edges and sharp needles.

'Wait – did anyone bring something to keep a needle in once we steal it?' said Spike.

The monsters looked at each other for an answer. Clearly, none of them had thought of this.

'Well, we have to contain it inside something. You know what happens when we touch those things.'

'Oooh. What exactly does happen when we touch it?' asked Hoot, only to be answered by a stern glare from the rest of the monsters.

'Ah, I see I've annoyed you by asking that question, which leads me to assume I've been told the answer before.'

'Correct,' hissed Miser.

'I knew it!' said Hoot triumphantly.

'Crush, go and find someting to keep the needle in once we nick it,' said Stan.

'HONK! HONK!' said Crush, scampering away at top speed.

'And how exactly do we "nick" it? I mean, there's people everywhere and it's trapped inside that glass case,' said Spike.

'Easy. Shove everyone out the way, smash it open, steal the needle, job done,' said Stan while cracking his knuckles. The other monsters erupted in protest.

'No, no, no, no, Stan! We must take more care,' hissed Miser.

'All right. Who's got a better plan then?'

The monsters fell silent as they considered the question.

'Well?' said Stan, his arms folded across his chest, his right hoof tapping impatiently.

The monsters thought as hard as they could, scratching their heads and pacing the corner of the room.

'So? Ideas? Anyone? Eh?' Stan was becoming more irritated and more impatient with every passing second. Of all the monsters, he feared saying goodbye to Nelson the most, and his fear had made him more anxious than a bee in a jar.

'We could set off the fire alarm, right? Clear the room of people first,' suggested Puff.

'LET'S JUST DO IT!!' roared Stan, before turning and smashing his fist into the panel of light switches on the wall. There was a loud bang, sparks flew from the panel, and the entire room was plunged into darkness. The

visitors responded with
shouts of surprise.

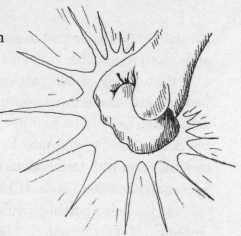

'Whatcha do dat
for?' exclaimed Nosh.

'He's flipped out,'
said Spike.

'My plan, my rules,'
said Stan, who set off
through the panicked
visitors towards the sin
extractor. He was so afraid of the
pain he would feel when having to say goodbye to Nelson
that he just wanted it over with as quickly as possible.
The other monsters chased after him. 'Besides, creates a
distraction, dunnit?' shouted Stan.

'Stan! You are not thinking clearly,' shouted Miser as
he dodged an elderly couple stumbling towards the exit.

'You know what Stan's like. Once he's fired up, there's
no reasoning with him,' moaned Spike. He had flattened
himself against the wall to avoid pricking the visitors who
were rushing around in all directions.

'Stay back!' cried Stan, who was now standing on top
of the perspex box containing the sin extractor.

'No! Wait! Crush isn't back yet! We need something
to keep the needle in!' wailed Puff, but it was too late.
With a manic expression on his big, red face, Stan held
his fists together above his head, and then brought them
down in a mighty hammer blow, smashing a hole in the

plastic. Visitors screamed in response to the loud *BANG* and cowered as shards exploded in all directions.

Unfortunately, in his haste to get the job done, Stan had forgotten about the powerful magnetic pull of the sin extractor. The hole he had just created exposed him to the needles below, and now he was being pulled down towards them with tremendous force.

'Aaaargh!' roared Stan as his right arm was sucked through the hole up to his shoulder.

'Quick! Take my hand!' Miser reached out one of his long tentacles towards Stan. The other monsters instinctively took hold of Miser in an attempt to anchor him to the ground.

Stan groaned and reached out his left hand towards Miser's tentacle. His right hand gripped one of the extractor needles.

'Pull!' said Miser, and the monsters pulled him with all their might. Stan gripped Miser's tentacle, which began to stretch like a rubber band. Stan was now in the middle of a tug of war between the sin extractor and his five monster friends.

'Pull harder!' shouted Stan.

'We're trying!' cried Spike.

Stan felt the needle in his right hand break loose from the sin extractor, and with all of his remaining strength he heaved his right arm back through the hole and flung the needle towards his fellow monsters. It spun across the floor like a wayward compass needle – and would have jammed itself straight into Nosh's pink belly had it not been for the sudden return of Crush. Crush pounced on the needle, trapping it against the ground with a cuddly toy pigeon he had stolen from the gift shop. (Cuddly toys had already proven to be secure vessels to contain a sin-extractor needle and, apart from a toddler who clapped with delight at the sight of a toy pigeon flying very low to the ground, Crush had been successful in remaining unnoticed.)

'HOOOONK!' honked Crush, pointing at Stan.

I was not exaggerating when I said Stan had used all his remaining strength to pull the needle out: he really did have nothing left to give, which is why he was now being sucked back through the hole in the plastic cover.

'Stan!' cried Puff. 'Don't let go of Miser!' But it was too late. Stan did not have the strength to hold on to Miser's tentacle any longer, and he let go.

There was an awful squelching noise as Stan was sucked through the hole, followed by a loud hiss as his body fell across the needles.

'No, Stan! Noooo!' wailed Nosh.

'HOOOOOONK!' honked Crush.

The other monsters could not cry out, or even speak. They were stunned by the sight of Stan disintegrating on the bed of needles. The sin extractor shook as if it were hungrily consuming him, and only a few seconds later Stan had been completely sucked through the needles.

No, I'm not joking.

Stan really was gone.

UNCLE POGO AND
THE SOGGY HOUSE

At the exact same moment as Stan disappeared from existence, Nelson felt a sudden attack of anxiety, and ran his bicycle straight into a skip outside Uncle Pogo's house. There was a very loud *clang* of metal, but Nelson and his bicycle were unharmed.

Nelson was used to sharing his feelings with his monsters, no matter how far apart they were, but he had never experienced a feeling like this before. Feelings tended to creep up and linger, but this one had come and gone in seconds.

Weird.

Nelson shook his head and waited to feel something else, something that would make sense of that anxiety. The wind blew through the trees, a bird sang from a telephone line, and a car passed by, but Nelson didn't receive any new feelings from his monsters. Assuming it must have been a false alarm, he gave a big sniff and leaned his bike against his uncle's garden wall.

Uncle Pogo was a curious man.

And almost all the things he was curious about – from

ancient tribal masks to transistor radios – were piled high in his tiny front garden. The garden was not the usual place to find all of his belongings, but since the basement floor of his house had been flooded in the night, this was to be the temporary resting place of his bizarre collection. The fussy neighbours were not pleased.

'It's a sign,' said Doody, who was dragging a wet and ruined rug towards a rented skip when Nelson arrived at the house. 'The universe is telling your uncle to get rid of some o' this stuff. And he ruddy well better before he moves in with me!' Doody laughed at his own joke. Sometimes when people do this it is annoying, but with Doody it was always infectious.

Nelson laughed when it suddenly struck him why he had been summoned: he was going to be asked to help tidy up the mess. Nelson's heart sank. This was the last thing he wanted to do. He wanted to eat half a packet of biscuits and watch TV with his monsters, not start hauling wet junk up staircases.

'So what happened?' said Nelson, stepping over a pile of very old wooden skis.

'Ah, it was the drains, dear boy, the d-r-r-r-rains!' said Doody, rolling his rs. 'Pipe under this house must have been blocked for a while without Pogo knowing, and then boom! Pipe burst, and it overflowed in the night.'

'Nightmare,' said Nelson.

'Totally,' said Doody. 'And while Pogo's fiddling around getting his false leg back on, I go and lift the cover off the main drain, and I find that stinky little stone in the middle of all this gunk blocking the pipe.'

Nelson gasped. Doody had no idea that what he was pointing at was not just a smelly stone, but a Bang Stone: a magical element that could transport you wherever you wanted to go. Nelson could hardly believe what he was seeing. While Doody continued to chatter and move things out to the skip, Nelson took a closer look at the little stone that was vibrating, bubbles fizzing and popping on its surface. He had swallowed that very stone twice before. Once when it was given to him by fish as means to escape from being trapped underwater, and the second time to get back home from Brazil. But he hadn't come back home: he had arrived outside Pogo's house in the midst of a terrible rainstorm, and right there, in the street where the skip now sat, Nelson had coughed up the stone and it had fallen into the street. The rain had been falling hard and washed the stone . . . down the drain. The very same drain that ran beneath Pogo's house.

'Smells 'orrible, dunnit? Like rotten eggs.' Doody picked up the stone with gloved hands and tossed it into the skip.

Nelson looked at the skip, and felt a strong desire to jump in and rescue the stone.

'Nelson! *Hello!* Look! We've been flooded!' From the tone of his voice you would assume Uncle Pogo was delighted to see his home ruined. He was stomping out of the house wearing fly-fishing waders, a sweater from *The Phantom of the Opera*, and a sailor's cap. There was no need for the cap; he just thought it went with the waders.

'So you want me to help clear up, then?' said Nelson, trying (but failing) to sound positive.

'No, no, no! I've got something to show you! Wait right there.'

Nelson was relieved not be dragged into helping, and waited by the door while his uncle stomped into the house, and then stomped back out again, holding a small box.

'What is it?' said Nelson.

'Rings,' said Pogo excitedly, and he opened the box to reveal two silver rings.

'Cool,' said Nelson.

'They're our wedding rings. I realized we'd given your sister a role in the wedding as bridesmaid, and forgotten about you. So we thought it would be fun if you'd be our ring bearer. You know, give us the rings during the service?'

'But what if I mess it up?' Nelson already felt the pressure not to mess up.

'You won't mess it up. You just hang on to the rings

before the service and pass them to us when the time comes.

'Slightly scary, but OK.'

'Ha ha. Thanks, Nelson.'

'Fancy a cup o' tea, you two?' said Doody, walking over.

Uncle Pogo smiled. 'Oh. That'd be perfect.'

'Great. I'll have two sugars in mine,' said Doody.

'Oh! You cheeky old git!' said Pogo.

As they waited for the kettle to boil in the kitchen, Nelson and Uncle Pogo tucked into a packet of chocolate biscuits.

'There's a girl at my school, Katy Newman,' Nelson began. 'She's putting on a play – *Bugsy Malone*—'

'Oh, I love *Bugsy Malone*—'

'Yeah, and she wanted to know if you could help make her some splurge guns.'

'Look at your uncle's face,' said Doody, overhearing their conversation as he passed by with a box containing several pairs of Tibetan slippers, a Peruvian pan pipe and assorted martial arts weapons. 'Splurge guns? O' course he's gonna make you some splurge guns. Look at him. You've made his ruddy day, you 'ave!'

Nelson laughed, and Uncle Pogo watched Doody leaving through the front door, whistling as he went.

'Was it a bit of shock? You know, hearing about me and Doody wanting to get married?' said Uncle Pogo as he poured the hot water into the teapot.

'Uhhh. No. No. Well, a bit. Yeah I s'pose a bit. But I'm glad. We all are. It's brilliant news, Uncle Pogo.'

Uncle Pogo's eyes glistened. 'You've no idea how much it means to hear you say that, Nelson.'

It made Nelson feel awkward to see an adult become emotional in front of him, so he distracted himself by shoving a biscuit into his mouth.

'See, the thing is, you never know how much time you're gonna have together,' continued Pogo. 'And time is so precious, Nelson, so you just gotta make the most of it. You really do.'

Nelson nodded thoughtfully. The time he had left with his own monsters might be coming to an end, and they couldn't or, more to the point, *shouldn't* waste a single second of it. They had to make the most of it. They couldn't just end their time together being sad: they had to have some fun.

After a mug of very sweet tea and yet another chocolate cookie or biscuit, Nelson left Doody and Uncle Pogo heaving a roll of soggy carpet out of the basement, climbed into the skip and, after a bit of digging around, retrieved the Bang Stone. He wrapped it up in a plastic bag and stuffed it into his backpack. Nelson did not yet know exactly what he was going to do with the Bang Stone, but something in the back of his mind convinced him it could be used for something fun.

STAN 2.0

You are probably worried about what happened to Stan. Well this is what happened . . .

While Nelson had been talking with Doody and Pogo, a few miles away, inside the Museum of London, Stan had disintegrated, having been sucked into the sin extractor. It was his own fault for being hot-headed and not thinking about the consequences of his actions.

He had been reduced to his essence, which had then spilt from the base of the sin extractor into one of seven copper vials held underneath.

The visitors to the museum had left the room after the lights had gone out. Now the remaining six monsters watched with amazement as their angry red friend reappeared as vapour. At first, all that could be seen of him was steam rising from the copper vial. Then the vial shook, and toppled from the rack on to the floor.

'Look . . . at . . . that . . .' said Puff in awe.

'Wowzers . . .' exclaimed Hoot. 'Did we all look like that when we were born?'

At first, Stan was no more than a wriggling red blob the size of a tennis ball, with a lump growing out of the top of him. He grew quickly, the lump stretching and peeling like a banana to reveal a purple horn beneath, angry eyes popping out of the red flesh beneath, just as that distinctive surly mouth appeared.

'Honk!' said Crush, who thought this newborn version of Stan was adorable.

The smell of burned fireworks filled the air as two little fists punched their way out of the sides of the red blob and two little hooves kicked out of the bottom.

'Well, well, well,' said Spike, who rarely experienced joy but was certainly feeling it now. 'Look who it is! Little baby Stan.'

'Who you callin' a baby!? Eh?!' snapped Stan, who was now standing on two legs, looking exactly like he did before, only less than half his original size.

The six monsters burst into hysterics – for Stan was not only smaller than before, his voice was high-pitched like a chipmunk.

'What happened to me? What's happened to my voice?! What's going on?!' Stan was only now realizing he was the same height as Crush.

'Baby Stan! Dat is da funniest fing I ever see in my whole life!' laughed Nosh.

'Shut ya face, ya big pink blob!' squeaked Stan, but this only made the monsters laugh even more. Miser took it upon himself to explain. 'You went through the sin extractor and out the other side.'

'What?' said Stan, his eyes wide with shock.

Miser waved the toy pigeon at him impatiently.'I can explain in greater detail later, but we have what we came for and I suggest we leave at once.'

'But I'm tiny! I'm flippin' half the size I was before!'

'You seem not to have lost any of your anger, though. In fact, it appears you are merely a concentrated version of your previous self,' observed Miser.

The monsters roared with laughter, which made Stan stomp his little feet and growl like a lion.

'I say we go . . . before he does a Rumpelstiltskin . . . and stomps a hole in the floor,' said Puff, smirking.

'Who you callin' Rumpelstiltskin!?' said Stan menacingly.

'Well, I think you look pretty nifty that size,' said Hoot to Stan as they ran back towards the museum exit.

'Shut ya beak, ya feather-brain,' snapped Stan.

On the bus ride back to Ivan's house, the monsters realized that Stan 2.0 was not to be messed with. Even though he had succeeded in retrieving a sin-extractor needle, the reason they had come to the museum in the first place, Stan was more furious than any of the monsters had seen him before. Miser had been right: Stan really was a more concentrated version of himself – his skin redder, his horns a more vivid purple, his temper quicker, his frustration greater, his glare more intense.

THE WISH LIST

It was just after 6 p.m. when Nelson arrived at Ivan's house. Ivan came out of the workshop to meet him and closed the door behind him.

They say they are very upset, signed Ivan, sighing worriedly.

I know, signed Nelson. *So am I.*

Ivan moved forward and gave Nelson a hug, patting his back in a firm and friendly way to avoid it feeling too sentimental. Ivan was good at reading people's feelings and knowing just what they needed in that moment. Right then he knew Nelson was close to tears, but would have felt ashamed to cry in front of Ivan, so a brotherly hug was just the thing. Reassuring but not overwhelming.

I'm going to leave you all alone.

Thank you.

Ivan showed Nelson inside, where he found all seven of his monsters wearing gloves and sitting on the floor beside the wood burner, staring at the flames.

'Stan?' said Nelson in surprise. 'What the heck happened to you?'

'I don't wanna talk about it, all right?!' barked Stan,

and he stormed off past Nelson to sit on the other side of the workshop.

'He's tiny! What did you do to him?' asked Nelson of the other monsters.

Between them they told Nelson about their day; how they had sneaked into the museum to steal a sin-extractor needle; and how Stan had wound up passing through the device.

'So the needle you stole is inside that?' asked Nelson, pointing at the cuddly pigeon beside Crush.

They all nodded in response.

'And, what? I just stick that needle into my skin and you all go back inside me?'

They all nodded again.

Nelson still didn't think he could let this happen. He wasn't ready to let them go. But he decided to play along for the time being.

'CAN WE JUST GET IT OVER WITH COS I CAN'T STAND THIS WAITIN' AROUND!' bellowed Stan from across the room. He had tears in his eyes, and his teeth were clenched.

'No, we are not just going to "get it over with". I was just at Uncle Pogo's house, and he was saying this thing about how time is precious and you've got to make the most of it.'

'Uncle Pogo's right,' said Puff with a sigh.

'Exactly, so before you all go – you know, before we have to say goodbye to each other forever – let's make the most of it; let's have an absolutely wicked time,' said Nelson, swinging his backpack from his shoulder and on to the floor.

'What? Are we gonna have a party?' Spike could not have sounded more sour. 'Celebrate how rubbish it is that we have to leave?'

'Nope!' said Nelson cheerfully as he rummaged around in his backpack. 'I had this idea on the way over. Each one of you gets to pick something you want to do. Absolutely anything in the whole world. Like a wish. And we do it. Whatever it is.' Nelson pulled the Bang Stone out of the backpack.

'Ooooooh!' groaned Nosh at the smell of the stone.

'A Bang Stone,' whispered Miser, his fingers flexing as they reached out towards it.

'I'd recognize that eggy stink from anywhere,' moaned Spike.

'I found it at my uncle's house. It's the same one I used to get home that time we saved my sister. Remember?'

They all nodded. How could they forget?

'Well, we can go anywhere in the world with this. Anywhere! And you're all invisible, and as long as I am too, we can do anything we want – right?'

'Can you make me big again?' growled Stan from the corner of the room.

'I'm not a genie, Stan. Whatever you want to do, it has to actually exist somewhere – it has to be real. But it can be anything. So? If you could go anywhere or do anything in the world, what would it be?'

The mood in the workshop swiftly changed from glum to giddy as Nelson began to make a list of each monster's name and the thing they most wanted to do.

It turned out to be the most extraordinary list you have ever seen.

THE MET GALA

Only the most famous, most fabulous, most beautiful, most exciting people are invited to the Met Gala in New York City. It is *the* fashion event of the year, and every guest makes a special effort to dress up in something they hope will impress their peers and send people on social media websites clicking the LIKE button in their millions. Pop stars have been known to arrive in gowns so huge that it takes a team of people to help them up the stairs. A movie star once arrived with a replica of his own head under his arm. Glamour, glitz and wild invention are celebrated here, and so it should be no surprise to learn that it was Hoot's wish to attend the Met Gala.

It had been Celeste's idea to activate the Bang Stone at the bottom of Ivan's garden, since it backed on to a train track and the sound of a passing train would help cover the loud bang of their departure.

The train approached.

The monsters crowded together.

Miser swallowed the Bang Stone, closed his eyes and pictured the location they intended to go to in his mind.

BANG!

Celeste and Ivan took off their safety goggles and stared at the patch of ground where her brother and his monsters had been standing only seconds before.

'Wow,' said Ivan with a chuckle of disbelief as he crouched and pressed his palm into the grass.

BANG!

Nelson and his monsters were relieved to find they were alone on the roof of the Metropolitan Museum of Modern Art and crawled to the edge. Fortunately, New York is a very noisy city and the constant symphony of motor engines, police sirens, construction sites and car horns meant no one heard the *bang*. Nelson's monsters cooed at the sight of the city. It may have been noisy, but it was breathtakingly beautiful.

'That's it, the Met Gala, exactly what you wished for, Hoot,' said Nelson proudly as he peered down at the guests posing on the red carpet for the paparazzi. 'Now, Hoot, remember the plan. We'll wait for you here, and if you start to swell up in size, get out of there straight away.'

Nelson turned round to find Hoot had already gone. Unable to contain his excitement, Hoot had flown down the side of the building in order to join the party.

It was the most impressive entrance anyone had ever seen in the history of the Met Gala. Swooping low over the heads of the world's press came a single white sheet, like a cheap Halloween ghost costume. It landed right in front of the paparazzi, where it stood very still for a few seconds.

Who on earth is this? people asked one other. *Who is under the sheet? How did they manage to fly over our heads?*

When you're looking to make an entrance, surprise is everything. Hoot knew this only too well, which is why he waited under the sheet for a few more seconds before revealing himself to the world.

Whoosh! Hoot flung the sheet to one side and the cameras began a flashing frenzy. Onlookers screamed with delight, and the eyes of fellow guests almost popped out of their sockets as this extraordinary person paraded up and down the red carpet.

Like all of Nelson's monsters, Hoot was invisible. Dressing up was the only way to be seen by humans and dressing up was Hoot's speciality. Tonight Hoot had covered his body in golden glitter so that every feather shone and sparkled. Even his beak was coated in glitter, and upon his head he wore his favourite top hat, also given the golden glitter treatment. Ski goggles sprayed gold and encrusted with plastic gemstones covered his eyes, golden foil coated his teeth, and the only parts of Hoot that did not look like a bird were his hands (gloved) and his legs. Ivan had helped make Hoot a pair of stilts, over which he wore a pair of golden trousers and thigh-high golden boots. The stilts made Hoot appear to be a normal human being wearing a magnificent golden bird costume.

Over here! Hey! Look over your shoulder! To the right! Here! Here! One more please! The paparazzi screamed their requests at Hoot, who was only too happy to oblige each one of them with pose after pose.

'My dears, it is such an honour to be here among you tonight!' cried Hoot, though no one heard a word he said. He strutted up and down the steps soaking up applause from everyone, including Beyoncé and Jay-Z, who Hoot was thrilled to see were deeply impressed by him. He could have paraded all night and never got tired of the adulation, but reality started to catch up with Hoot. Security men began to take a serious interest in this strange guest who had arrived without a ticket. Hoot had made his way into the lobby of the museum, where fashion legend Anna Wintour insisted on having a picture taken of them both. With one final wave to the cameras, and a kiss he blew directly to Rihanna (who pretended to catch it), Hoot stepped into the elevator and pressed the button for the top floor.

Three security guards decided that although Hoot appeared to pose no threat to the Gala, they should pursue him just in case. They took the second elevator, and when they arrived on the top floor, they followed the trail of golden glitter through a fire-exit door and up on to the roof of the building.

BANG!

The loud noise made the security men drop to the ground, fearing it was a gun shot, but when they looked up, there was no sign of anyone else on the roof. The mysterious guest had vanished, leaving only a flurry of golden glitter in his wake.

GOLD FEVER

Nelson's plan was already working well. Creating a wish list for his monsters had given them all something to look forward to, instead of dwelling on the inevitable sadness of having to say goodbye.

Three days had passed since Hoot had graced the carpet of the Met Gala but he was still trending higher online than a new royal baby. No one knew Hoot's name, who he was or where he had come from. All anyone knew for sure was that someone dressed to look like a golden bird had been the star of the Met Gala and the mystery around this person only made the story more delicious.

Hoot had been banned from social media because one look at himself on Instagram made him quickly swell in size and this was very dangerous, especially when they were all inside Ivan's workshop and could easily be crushed.

'It was the greatest night of my entire life and I shall not forget it as long as I live,' croaked Hoot, who had lost his voice from all the singing and chatting he had been doing since the event.

'Well, you're not gonna live much longer, are ya?

We're all goin' back into Nelson, so enjoy it while it lasts, ya vain pillock!' snapped little Stan, who was stomping around the workshop looking for something to kick.

'Oh, but my image shall live on forever. Yes, I have been made . . . What's the word for someone that lives forever?'

'Immortal?' said Nelson.

'That's it! I am immortal!'

'You are a prat!' snapped Stan.

'All right, easy, Stan,' said Nelson. 'It's Miser's turn tonight. OK, Miser? Ready to go?'

'I am indeed, Master Nelson,' said Miser as he opened the door of the workshop to the garden.

BANG!

Nelson and his monsters opened their eyes to find they were standing in total darkness. He could hear Miser retch and throw up the stone, which clattered and fizzed on the ground.

'Someone find a light switch,' whispered Nelson as he reached out for something to hold on to. The monsters were pushing and shoving around him when he heard the whip-crack of Miser's tentacles, followed by a *click*. Dazzling fluorescent lights burst into life above him.

'Oow!' moaned Spike as he and the other monsters covered their eyes from the painfully bright light.

'You could have warned us, Miser! Instead of blinding us all, ya great blue berk!' squeaked little Stan.

But Miser didn't apologize. He had been struck dumb by the sight that stretched out before them: 500,000 bars of gold.

'Holy cow,' whispered Nelson. They had transported themselves to the vaults beneath the Bank of England. It was Miser's wish to be completely immersed in wealth, and here, in the second largest vault in the world, was enough gold to buy your own country.

'You can look, you can touch, but you cannot steal any of this,' were Nelson's orders. He was wearing his Mexican wrestler's mask, a precaution he always took in case of security cameras.

Miser remained speechless. His eyes were wide and his tentacles shivered with delight at the sight of gold bars stacked high in every direction.

'Diss is well borin',' said Nosh.

'Yeah . . . it's just a load of . . . metal,' said Puff with a yawn.

Crush felt equally bored, climbing into Nelson's arms and closing his eyes.

Miser was the only monster impressed by their surroundings. He walked slowly down the aisle, mesmerized. 'Mmm . . . gold . . .' he wheezed. He took a deep breath through those wide nostrils, licking his lips while his rubbery little fingers stroked the golden bars. Imagine you were very hungry and you found yourself surrounded by your favourite cakes. You would probably find it hard to resist eating one of the cakes, or at least

71

taking a nibble of the icing. But would you stop at just a nibble? Do you have that much self-control when it comes to something you crave? Miser felt equally conflicted around all this gold. He wanted it very, very much, and the deeper he walked into the vault, the greater his desire for the gold became.

'Imagine what one could buy with all of this gold? Everything, *everything* your heart desired . . .' whispered Miser to himself.

'All right, don't go too far. Maybe just stay up this end,' called Nelson, but Miser could not hear him over his own wheezing breath and thumping heart.

'Miser!? Did you hear me? I said, don't go too far!'

Miser stopped walking. His right hand gripped a bar of gold, and slowly he lifted it from the stack. His breathing became louder and faster, his eyes wider and more manic.

'Hey! Put that back!'

Too late. Miser was overcome with greed and began to pull the gold towards him.

'Hey! What are you doing!?' yelled Nelson as he started running towards Miser, dropping the snoozing Crush.

'Yes, what exactly is Miser up to? Is he making some sort of nest?' said Hoot.

Clang! Clang! Clang! went the gold as Miser pulled bar after bar off the shelves and piled them around himself.

'He's gone mad!' shouted Stan.

'Nelly-son, be careful!' cried Nosh.

Miser's rubbery tentacles were whipping around so

fast that Nelson couldn't get close to him.

'Gold fever!' shouted Spike. 'He's got gold fever!'

'What's gold fever?' replied Nelson.

'I don't know, I just made it up – but look at him! That's what he's got!'

Miser certainly looked like he had a fever. His blue skin was covered in a sheen of sweat, the whites of his eyes were bloodshot, his pupils dilated, his breathing fast, his mouth open, and drool ran down his chin as he collected the bars.

'GOLD!' roared Miser.

'You're gonna bury yourself alive under that stuff!' Nelson cried, but again, Miser didn't hear him. The tower of gold kept growing around him.

'Nosh! Throw me the Bang Stone!' said Nelson.

Nosh passed the stone to Stan, who threw it to Nelson. Nelson put the stone in his mouth and leaped at Miser.

BANG!

Celeste and Ivan came running out of the workshop to find Nelson wrestling with something invisible in the garden.

'You weren't supposed to come back here! We all agreed it was safer for you to come to the park! That bang's probably woken up the whole street,' said Celeste.

'It was an emergency!' said Nelson 'Miser went nuts! I think it was the gold. There was too much of it, and it made him freak out.' What Celeste and Ivan couldn't see was Miser lying on his back, pinned down by Nelson. He was frothing at the mouth and shaking violently. The whites of Miser's eyes had turned gold, and Nelson could see little golden veins threaded beneath his blue skin.

'It's OK – it's OK, Miser. Calm down. Just breathe. Everything's OK now. You just overdid it, that's all. It was too much. But you're safe now. We're home. We're back home. Shhh.'

To Nelson's relief, Miser's breathing slowed.

'Nelse, I think this has to stop now,' said Celeste. 'You can't keep exploding here in the back garden, even when there is a train coming.'

Nelson let go of Miser, who rolled on to his side and closed his eyes.

'But I've got to go back for the others,' said Nelson, panting heavily and reaching out for the Bang Stone in the grass.

'Well, after that you can't do it again. Seriously. That bang will have people calling the police.'

Before Nelson could answer, the train used to carry construction materials at night roared past – an enormous

74

stroke of luck, as this would surely cover the sound of the Bang Stone.

'Miser, wait here. I'll be right back,' he said.

BANG! The sound was buried beneath the loud clatter of the passing night train.

Miser coughed and spluttered in the grass.

'What happened? Where is Nelson? Where are the others?' he said breathlessly, but Celeste could not see or hear him to answer his questions.

BANG!

Nelson reappeared in the vaults to find his remaining six monsters running around in a blind panic. Blue lights were flashing in the ceiling and an alarm was ringing so loudly it felt as if the sound were drilling into his ears. Before he could breathe, Nelson had to throw up the stone. It clattered on the floor and Nelson wiped his mouth.

'Look out! Behind you!' yelled Puff, and Nelson turned to see three security guards running towards him.

'Aaaargh!'

Nelson ran as fast as he could in the opposite direction, completely forgetting about the Bang Stone. The guards would have caught him within seconds had it not been for Stan, who ran out in front of the men and knocked them off their feet.

Nelson tripped over too, though it was gold bars, not a monster, that caused him to fall.

'Jump on Nelly-son!' Nosh instructed.

'What are you doing?! I can't get up!' cried Nelson as his monsters piled on top of him. Nosh was last to join the pile, and just as the security guards were about to reach them, Nosh popped the Bang Stone in his mouth.

BANG!

THE MANGO FIASCO

Nelson knew they had escaped from the vault, but it wasn't until his monsters clambered off him that he could lift his head and see where they were. Though the sun had yet to rise, there was enough light in the sky to reveal rows and rows of leafy trees stretching out before them. Where the rows of trees ended, a dense and dark jungle spread beneath a smoking volcano.

'Where are we, Nosh?' said Nelson.

Nosh spat out the Bang Stone and gazed up at the leafy canopy of the tree they were all lying beneath. 'Mmmm...' He hummed. 'Mangoes.'

'What do you mean, mangoes? Nosh, where have you brought us?' said Nelson as he sat up, his head turning left and right, still half expecting to see security guards running towards him.

'Ooooo, diss was ma dream, Nelly-son. Remember? It was on da list. To come eat da mangoes from da mango trees. Me love da mangoes so muchly.'

Stan slapped Nosh's belly. 'You were *supposed* to take us back home! And this ain't home, is it?!' Stan picked up a broken wooden fruit crate with a picture of a mango and sunshine on the side. 'It's a flipping mango farm!' Stan threw the fruit crate on the ground and smashed it to bits.

The other monsters groaned and grumbled. After a scare like they'd had in the vaults, everyone wanted to be safely back at home and not on the other side of the world, no matter how good the fruit was.

'I must say, I find the sight of that volcano gives me the heebie-jeebies. Remember what happened to Buzzard and his monster? How they perished in the lava? Yikes.' Hoot shifted uneasily from foot to foot.

'Hooonk,' said Crush sadly as he remembered the adorable cuddly rhino leaping into the volcano.

Nelson pulled off his Mexican wrestler mask. The tropical heat was already making him drip with sweat. 'Nosh.' He sighed. 'We were going to do your wish another night. This was Miser's night, not yours.'

'And what's more, my dear Nosh, I'm afraid I don't see a single mango up here,' said Hoot, who had flown up on to a low branch.

'What?!' barked Nosh. 'Where all da mangoes gone!?'

Spike picked up what looked like a melted brown shoe

but was actually a rotten mango. 'I think we've missed the harvest.'

Stan began to chuckle.

'Nah, nah, nah, dere's gotta be da mangoes here! Me dream about comin' to diss place!' Poor Nosh looked around and realized that Spike was right. The trees had been harvested of all their fruit.

'Should have been here a month ago, it would've been ideal,' said Spike. 'Well, for you at least. Not for me. I don't really like mangoes. I prefer a banana, though I don't like it when they have brown squashy bits, or if they're too green, and I don't like the stringy bits you have to peel off. Come to think of it, I don't really like bananas.'

'Oh, will you stop moaning about bananas and let's just go home.' Stan punched the tree and the branches shook.

Nelson could see Nosh was fed up. 'Nosh, don't worry. We can do something else for you. But tonight is not the night. Let's just go back home, please.'

Nosh nodded reluctantly and picked up the Bang Stone that fizzed in the grass beside him.

'Everybody hold on,' said Nelson. There were no protests as they had all had enough adventures for one night and home was exactly where they wanted to be.

Nosh popped the stone into his mouth and closed his eyes.

BANG!

They were gone.

A MUMF AGO

BANG!

They were back under the mango tree.

Only now it was raining hard enough to hammer a nail into a plank of wood, and thunder was rumbling loudly in the sky above.

'What the heck are we doing here again?!' yelled Stan. The others groaned and sighed and shoved Nosh around for being such an idiot.

Nelson was so disorientated he couldn't speak. You have to remember that all of this has happened in just a few seconds. They were in the gold vaults of London, then they were under a mango tree in the early morning, and now they were beneath the same mango tree sheltering from an extremely heavy rainstorm.

'I must say, I am very confused. Was it not the plan to go back home?'

'Course it was, Hoot!'

'Mangoes!' roared Nosh triumphantly. He was bobbing up and down and looking up into the branches of the tree.

'I say, Nosh is absolutely right. Look at this! Mangoes galore!' said Hoot as he flew into the branches and brought a mango down from the tree in his beak. Nosh grabbed it from Hoot and ate greedily.

'Mmmm,' groaned Nosh, his eyes rolling back in their sockets as he savoured the delicious fruit.

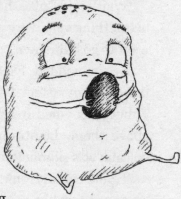

'What is going on? How did you make mangoes just appear like that? Nosh? How come there's a storm now?' asked Nelson.

Nosh took a break from eating to speak. 'I was just a-wishin' I was here a mumf ago for da mangoes and here we is – a mumf ago,' he said as if it were no big deal.

'We've gone back in time? Seriously? And all to get a fresh mango?!' said Nelson.

'Well, well, I didn't know time travel was possible,' said Hoot.

'Neither . . . did any of us,' said Puff, arching his back and widening his eyes. 'I don't like it. We've . . . we've crossed some kind of line . . . It's freaking me out.' Puff's fur was standing on end.

A little ball of anxiety started to grow in Nelson's stomach. 'Puff's right. This is wrong. This feels really, really wrong. We should not have done this.'

'Izz not wrong, izz delish!' said Nosh, licking his lips as he tucked into his fourth mango.

'Nosh, you have got to stop thinking with your stomach,' said Nelson. 'Give me the stone.'

'Wait!' said Spike, holding up his scrawny hands. 'You better think very, very carefully about not just *where* you want to go but *when*.'

Nelson nodded. Except for Nosh, who was still eating, the other monsters fell silent and watched him think. Thunder boomed overhead. The rain pounded the tree above them. Lightning flashed and for a second the volcano was silhouetted against the clouds.

'Honk! Honk! Honk!' said Crush as he hugged Nelson's leg to comfort him.

'OK, I'm ready. Just hold on tight, everyone,' said Nelson, and they all did – even Nosh, his mouth overflowing with mango juice.

Nelson closed his eyes, put the revolting stone in his mouth, and *BANG!* They were gone.

The train used to carry construction materials at night roared past the end of Ivan's garden.

'Miser, wait here. I'll be right back,' said Nelson.

BANG! The sound was buried beneath the loud clatter of the passing night train.

Miser coughed and spluttered in the grass.

'What has happened to me? Where is Nelson? Where are the others?' he said breathlessly, but Celeste could not see or hear him to answer his questions.

You may be thinking that you have read these lines

before, and you are right. It all happened a few minutes ago, and it was precisely this time that Nelson was returning to.

BANG!

Celeste stepped back in shock. 'That was quick! Are you OK? Why are you soaking wet?'

Nelson blinked the rainwater out of his eyes and turned to face his sister.

'Oh, it's good to be back,' he said with a great sigh, and collapsed with relief on the grass next to Miser.

THE INCREDIBLE EFFECTS
OF SUPER-SLEEP

Since the mango fiasco, Nelson had had to concentrate harder than ever before at school. No matter what lesson he had, even rugby practice, Nelson found his thoughts drifting back to the night under the mango tree. How strange it was to have travelled through time. It dawned on him that he now possessed the power to go back to any point in history. He could use it to answer questions no one on earth knew the answers to. Photograph real dinosaurs. Meet the very first human beings. Shake hands with Jesus. Find out exactly why and how Stonehenge came to be. And could he travel into the future too, he wondered? Could he see what would become of the world? Did we find a solution to global warming? Would he grow up to be a happy man? Could he discover secrets and bring them home, make himself rich?

As the possibilities of time travel opened up before him, so too did the same uneasy feeling he had had beneath the mango tree. Time travel was a scary prospect. To travel through time meant you had to detach from reality. There would always be a risk of not being able to get back to the present. And if there was one thing he had learned in the last few days, it was just how precious the present was. The thought of being lost in time made Nelson shiver, and that shiver was his subconscious mind's way of telling him to never, ever, *ever* travel through time again.

'Well, I'm glad you're not going to use the Bang Stone any more,' said Celeste as she hammered a tent peg into the grass. 'It's freaky enough to see your brother disappear, but that noise, that massive bang, it's really scary.'

Nelson pulled the cord attached to the top of the tent and tied it to Celeste's tent peg.

'Yep. My monsters agree. None of them want to use it any more. And I'm glad Puff's wish can just happen here in the garden.'

They had finished pitching the tent at the bottom of Nelson's family garden. The sun had set, dinner had been eaten, and their parents were inside watching the news. George, the boy next door, was bouncing up and down on his trampoline but could not see Nelson's tent as it was pitched behind the garden shed.

'What time are your monsters coming over?' whispered Celeste as she looked at her watch.

'They're already here,' said Nelson.

'I'm going . . . to put us all . . . into a kind of super-sleep,' said Puff a little later, and he yawned an infectious yawn that the other monsters and Nelson replicated. They were all crammed into the tent, Nelson in his pyjamas and tucked into his sleeping bag, with Crush snuggled beside him and Puff spread out on his chest.

'Super-sleep? Don't like the sound of that,' mumbled Stan, who was fidgeting close to Nelson's feet.

'Don't worry . . . the only side effects . . . are that you wake up . . . feeling lovely . . . and if we go into super-sleep . . . I can join us all up . . . in the same dream . . .' Puff was smiling, delighted to be getting his wish.

'It sounds like just the rest we need,' said Miser, who coughed and shivered. He had not been the same since the gold fever, and there were still little flecks of gold in his eyes.

'The rest *you* need, ya greedy git,' snapped Stan.

'All right. Let it rip, Puff,' said Nelson, but instead of farting out a cloud of gas as he usually did, Puff belched. It was an extremely long belch that made everyone laugh out loud. A glittering lavender-scented purple cloud bloomed out of Puff's mouth, filling the tent, and as it settled upon Nelson and his monsters, their laughter faded and they fell into a deep sleep.

The sun was shining. Nelson was wearing his red swimming shorts. His skin had been browned by the sun. He jumped from the black rock he was standing on and for a few seconds he was airborne before he crashed into the cool blue sea. A curtain of bubbles rose around him and when it lifted he could see as clearly as he could on land. Fish surrounded him. They were happy to see him.

So was Miser, who Nelson could see looking up at him cheerfully from the ocean floor.

'Miser! I can see underwater,' said Nelson to Miser.

'You can speak underwater too,' said Miser.

'Oh yeah!'

Splash! Crush, Stan, Puff and Nosh had jumped from the rock and arrived beside him.

Nelson laughed. 'This doesn't feel like a dream. It feels totally real!'

'I knew you'd like it,' said Puff with a grin.

'Lezz go!' shouted Nosh, and he swam down deeper into the water, his little legs kicking furiously behind him.

For what felt like an entire day, Nelson and his monsters swam and played in their own private cove on the beach of their dreams. When they were hungry, food would appear upon a blanket laid out on the sand. Doughnuts and peach ice tea and ice cream and mangoes and a never-ending bowl of sweet chilli-flavoured crisps. Whatever they thought of, it appeared. When they were too hot, a cool breeze would blow. When Stan suggested they play Frisbee, a Frisbee popped out of a rock like toast from a toaster. Hoot flew in joyous circles in the sky, leaving a multicoloured trail in his wake. Spike sat in the shade beneath the rock enjoying the sensation of butterflies landing on the end of his cactus needles.

And while they dreamed together, their real bodies lay fast asleep inside the tent at the bottom of Nelson's garden. Their hearts beat in time with each other. Their lungs breathed in time with each other. Puff was stretched out on top of Nelson like a living, breathing blanket. His purple fur glistened and sparkled, and as the joy of their collective dream increased, Puff grew. Well, he didn't just get bigger; he started to inflate. Gradually he began to float away from Nelson until he was pressed against the roof of the tent, like a furry purple balloon.

CLOUD NINE

We all know how lovely it feels to have had a good night's rest, but Nelson had never experienced a sleep like this. Every single part of his body and his mind felt brand new, and the dream they had all shared had been such a happy one that he could barely stop smiling for five days afterwards. Even the knowledge that there were only three wishes left to go before they had to say goodbye to each other forever could not wipe that smile off Nelson's face.

His school work improved so much and so quickly that his teachers started to talk about him on their coffee break.

'Have you noticed a change in Nelson Green? He's never been interested in my lesson before, but for the last few days he's been my best student.'

'He's gone from bottom to the top of my class.'

'You know, he helped carry my books to my car, and I must say I never knew he could be such a chatty little fellow. Always thought of him as a quiet one.'

'He's reminded me of his sister recently. Do you remember her? Celeste. Delightful girl.'

And it wasn't just the teachers who had seen a sudden change in Nelson. Nelson's classmates couldn't fail to notice how instead of slinking into the classroom and flopping down into a seat, Nelson now bounded in, humming a tune he had heard on the radio and chatting to anyone who was nearby.

'What's happened to you?' whispered Katy Newman one day, as if the answer might be a secret.

'Nothing.'

'Then why are you so . . . so up?'

They were sitting on the swings in the playground at break-time. Nelson shrugged as he ate the rest of his Lion bar. 'Dunno. Oh! I totally forgot to tell you. My Uncle Pogo's already made a prototype splurge gun and he sent a video to see if you like it.' Nelson pulled his phone out of his backpack, switched it on and showed Katy the video. It started with a clip of a large black toy Nerf gun lying on a workbench. Pogo's voiceover explained he had sprayed the gun black and added a small compressed air tank to the shaft, which was connected to a liquid foam dispenser. Then the picture cut to a shot of him holding the gun and pointing it at Doody in their living room.

'It has a good range, probably about six metres, but it is completely safe,' said Uncle Pogo.

'It better be!' snapped Doody.

'Three . . . two . . . one . . .' *Pop!* Pogo fired the gun and Doody's face was instantly coated in a thick layer of white foam.

Katy burst into hysterics while on the video Pogo laughed at the sight of Doody shaking his head and wiping the foam out of his eyes.

'Oh my gosh, your uncle is a genius!'

Nelson felt very proud to be Pogo's nephew but their sudden outburst of laughter had drawn attention from everyone in the playground, including Mr Mallison, who was on break duty.

'Pogo said if you're happy with it he will be able to make twelve of them,' said Nelson as he hid his phone from sight. He was way more enthusiastic about Katy's play since the super-sleep, and had even agreed to play Bugsy.

'Of course I'm happy with it!' squealed Katy. 'Oh, this is going to be the best show ever!'

It wasn't just Nelson who had been on a high since the super-sleep. All of his monsters were happier than they had ever been, and Puff was literally high. Instead of crawling around on the floor, Puff now floated a metre from the ground. His body was rounder than it used to be, his paws dangled beneath him, and underneath those heavy-lidded eyes stretched a wide, satisfied grin that never left his face. When he needed to move, Puff could simply swim through the air like a dog in water. This change

in Puff meant the monsters could now get around more quickly. Instead of having to carry Puff or wait for him to catch up wherever they went, Miser could pull him along beside them like a balloon on the end of one of his long tentacles, and this was especially useful when it came to the night of honouring Crush's wish.

Crush was so excited about getting his wish, he had been making little honking noises all afternoon, though if you had seen how excited all the other monsters were, you would have assumed they were *all* getting their wish.

BANG!

THE ROCK

'We're ready for you on set, Mr Johnson,' said Lita, the film's second assistant director.

'Be right there, Lita,' said Dwayne 'The Rock' Johnson, who remembered the name of every single crew member despite there being hundreds of them. Lita closed the trailer door and radioed the first assistant director to say that Dwayne was seconds away, and for everyone to stand by on set.

The stunt drivers started their cars. The machine guns were primed and ready for firing. The pyrotechnics were switched from safe to standby mode in preparation for blowing up an entire warehouse as soon as Dwayne's car drove through the wall.

They had been filming in London for two weeks now, and crowds of fans had gathered every night at the security gates in the hope of catching a glimpse of the star. He would often say hello to them and take a few selfies with them before heading back to his hotel, but tonight Dwayne 'The Rock' Johnson was going to meet his biggest fans of all time.

*

There was a knock on the trailer door. Dwayne grabbed his jacket from the chair.

'Yeah, I know, I know, Lita. I'm coming.'

Dwayne opened the door to find he was looking down at seven monsters and a boy. Well, he could only see Nelson, which is just as well because all seven monsters lost their minds at the sight of him.

'HOOOOOOOOOONK!' blasted Crush as he bounced up and down and clapped his four hands.

'DA ROCK!' shouted Nosh.

'Look at him! Magnificent!' cried Hoot.

'He's a god,' whispered Puff.

'Indeed he is,' said Miser.

'Wish I had arms like that,' groaned Spike.

'HOOOOOOOOOOOONK!' wailed Crush. He was now shaking so violently that the other monsters had stepped away from him.

'I LOVE YOU TOO, DA ROCK!' shouted Nosh.

'Hello, Mr Rock,' began Nelson nervously, and Stan quickly corrected him.

'You call 'im "Mr Johnson", you numpty!'

'Sorry . . . Mr Johnson. We're big fans of yours – I mean, I'm a big fan of yours and I wondered if . . .'

'Better do this quickly, kid – they're waiting for me on set,' said Dwayne, turning back into his trailer to fetch a photo. His assistant made sure he always had plenty on standby as Dwayne was asked for an autograph a billion times a week.

'Come in,' he said to Nelson. When Nelson didn't budge, his monsters pushed him forward.

'Oopsie, watch the step there. Now, what's your name?' said Dwayne as he clicked the end of his pen.

'Crush . . .'

'Your name is Crush?'

'Uh, it's my nickname.'

'Cool nickname. Here, take a tissue. You've got some kinda sticky stuff on your jacket there.'

'Oh. Thanks. That's . . . weird,' said Nelson, pretending not to know where it had come from. Having hidden inside Nosh's belly to get past security meant he still had traces of stomach gloop stuck to his jacket.

As Dwayne wrote a little message and signed the photo, Crush rushed up to his left leg and very gently hugged it. Crush's little orange body shivered with delight and he let out a honk so deep that the trailer started to vibrate.

'Hooooooooooooonk.'

'Whoa, what was that?' said Dwayne, putting his hands on the table to feel the shake.

Nelson shrugged.

'Easy, Crush. Don't get overexcited,' said Spike.

'Oooh,' whispered Nosh at the sight of a large sneaker lying by the door. He licked his lips and said, 'Da Rock's shoe.' If Nelson had heard Nosh say this he would have taken action, but he was too busy smiling at Dwayne to notice Nosh gobbling up the movie star's sneaker.

'So, Crush, I guess if you got to my trailer you must know someone working on this movie,' said Dwayne.

'Uh, yes,' Nelson lied.

'Who is it?'

'Uh . . . Mo . . . lly . . . Hoo . . . shh . . . eemoo?'

'Molly Hooshimoo? I don't think I've met Molly.'

Nelson blushed bright pink.

'Molly *Hooshimoo*? What kinda name is that to come up with, you idiot!?' said Stan in an angry whisper.

'What does she do here?' asked Dwayne.

'Molly, she's, uh . . . she's . . .' Nelson was struggling to come up with an answer when a fireball erupted from the top of Nosh's head and hit the ceiling.

'AHH!' cried Dwayne, who tripped, fell backwards over Crush and smacked the back of his head on the corner of the kitchen table. He lay on the floor, knocked out cold.

'OH MY GOD!' cried Nelson. 'YOU'VE KILLED THE ROCK!'

'HONK!' screamed Crush, and the monsters went into panic mode.

Crush caressed the head of his beloved hero and honked into his ear.

'Get 'im some water!' ordered Stan, and Hoot did as instructed, flying over to collect a fish bowl containing three fish.

Splash! went the water and the little fish, all over Dwayne, Nelson and the carpet.

'Yeah, ideally without fish in it!' spluttered Nelson, collecting the poor things carefully as they flopped around on the floor and plopping them into a glass of water.

The water had no effect on Dwayne, and now the flames were spreading quickly across the ceiling, down the wall and into the small kitchen area.

'FIRE!' cried Nosh, and Miser's tentacles reached out to pull a fire extinguisher from the wall. He aimed it at the ceiling. *Fsssssshhhh!* went the extinguisher. Thick white foam appeared but it seemed no match for the growing fire.

Crush clung to Dwayne's now foam-soaked head and wailed. 'HOOOOOOOONK!'

'We've gotta get The Rock out!' cried Puff over all the shouting.

'YOU TAKE 'IS HEAD, I'LL TAKE 'IS FEET!' Stan commanded, and with that he dragged Dwayne's feet to the door and down the steps. Sadly, no one had responded quick enough to the command to hold Dwayne's head and so it bounced down the four trailer steps like a basketball with a face and landed – *splat!* – in a puddle of mud at the bottom.

'Do not worry. The fire is out, Master Nelson,' said

97

Miser as he stepped down from the trailer, covered in foam. Sadly, Miser could not have been more wrong. While he had succeeded in extinguishing the flames on the ceiling, the fire had also spread beneath the kitchen cupboards, where it met with a large gas canister and . . . *BOOM!* The back wall of the trailer blew away in a shower of sparks and sent the trailer shooting forwards like a rocket. Nelson's mouth fell open at the sight of Dwayne's trailer trundling down a dirt slope and gathering so much speed that when it reached the bottom, it drove right through a gigantic green-screen sheet that had been hung at the back of the location, rolled through a set that had been made to look like an airplane hangar, and smashed through the fake wall that Dwayne was supposed to be driving his stunt car through.

'Run!' cried Nelson, and they ran back towards the film-set fence. Hoot flew over Nelson's head, grabbed hold of his shoulders and pulled him up into the air and over the fence while the rest of the monsters ran through the security gate.

'SORRY, DA ROCK!' was all Nosh could think to say as he looked at their beloved action hero, for Nosh knew that had he not eaten the sneaker, his stomach would not have incinerated it, flames would not have shot from the top of his head, there would have been no fire, and Dwayne would now be looking fabulous while driving a car – and not lying unconscious in a puddle of mud covered in white foam while his trailer burned to a crisp in front of a stunned camera crew.

NOTE: you will be pleased to know that Dwayne 'The Rock' Johnson was only mildly concussed and will be returning to your screens very soon.

THE UNHAPPY VAN

Though their encounter with Dwayne 'The Rock' Johnson had not exactly gone to plan, Nelson and his monsters were still in a good mood. Crush had been especially happy and spent most of the next day staring at the signed photo, tracing the ink with his fingers as if this connected him to his idol.

As Nelson cycled back from the first rehearsal of Katy's play, however, he felt a sudden heavy feeling in his chest as he remembered there were only two monster wishes left: Spike's and Stan's. Both of these monsters had been tricky when it came to deciding what they wanted to do. Spike simply couldn't make up his mind, whereas Stan had lots of ideas, but they all involved getting revenge on someone who might have upset Nelson or caused him to feel shame in the past.

Nelson had refused to let Stan react to any of these incidents. 'It's not worth it, Stan; all these things bother you way more than they bother me. I mean, yes, it was embarrassing when those girls laughed at me at lunch today, but how was I supposed to know I had a massive bogey hanging out of my nose? And you can't just give the sports teacher a wedgie because he didn't allow a try in our last rugby game.'

'You lost the game cos of 'im!'

'*No*, we lost the game because the other team were a bit better than us.'

'Let me go after the captain of the other team. He was a nasty little cheat and he elbowed you in the face.'

'No, Stan! It was an accident! No revenge wishes, OK? You *have* to think of something else.' Though Nelson had been strict with Stan, he secretly loved how much Stan stood up for him. It was like having a tiny red bodyguard, which, though ridiculous, was actually a reassuring thing to have in his life.

As Nelson cycled along the cycle path, he noticed some of the passing cars had switched on their headlights, so he pulled over beside the park and switched on his lights too. A squealing sound caught Nelson's attention and, looking behind him, he saw a van pulling into the side of the road. It was a rusty, unhappy-looking vehicle and the van's engine made an awful, high-pitched whining noise. The handbrake crunched as the driver brought the van to a stop.

Nelson turned away, covering his mouth and nose with the crook of his arms to avoid breathing in the cloud of black petrol fumes. With one hand on the handlebars, he pushed off, but had only gone a few feet when a man shouted, 'Nelson? Nelson Green!'

Nelson was so shocked to hear his name he almost fell off his bike.

Stopping once again, he turned to see a male driver lean out of the window. He had light brown hair cut very short around his ears, small eyes and a smile just a little too wide for such a narrow face. He gave Nelson the creeps.

'Who are you?' shouted Nelson.

'Mate. Just wanna talk to you for a minute,' said the man and he opened the door of his van.

Nelson was standing out of his saddle and pedalling away at full speed before the man had even set foot on the ground. Talking with strangers made him feel uncomfortable at the best of times, but this stranger struck fear in Nelson's heart.

He shot across the park, past the basketball court, and straight through the adventure playground.

Down the alleyway, across the car park of the council estate, past kids with wet hair swinging their bags as they left the public pool, and on to the pavement past a row of small shops – Nelson knew he was going too fast to stop should someone suddenly appear, but his fear was as powerful as rocket fuel and there was no way he was going to slow down until he was safely back with his monsters.

It was only as he reached the smashed-up pub at the end of Ivan's road that Nelson dared to glance over his shoulder. No sign of the van. Nelson let out a great sigh of relief, sat down in the saddle and allowed the bike to coast the last few metres towards Ivan's house. His monsters were already rushing out to greet him.

'What 'appened? Why you all freaked out?' squeaked Stan.

Nelson dropped his bike to the ground and pulled out his phone. The rules were that he was never to talk directly to his monsters in public in case someone saw him and became suspicious, so pretending to talk on the phone was the agreed solution.

'Hi. How are you?' said Nelson into the phone.

'HONK! HONK! HONK!' Crush was running around in circles. You could see from the monsters' wide eyes and their jittering movements that Nelson's fear had infected them too.

'*How are we?* We felt what you felt and we were jolly well pooping our pants, dear boy!' said Hoot breathlessly.

'We don't wear any pants, you stupid bird!' snapped Stan.

'What has happened, Master Nelson? Do we need to prepare ourselves for bad news?' asked Miser.

'I'm OK – just had a bit of a creepy encounter with some van driver in the street.' As he pretended to talk on the phone, Nelson walked around the side passage and into Ivan's workshop.

'Right!' said Stan as he slammed the door behind them. 'Can you please tell us what exactly happened?'

WHO WAS THE MAN
IN THE VAN?

What Nelson didn't know was that the man in the van was called Jim Tindle. Jim was a pale-skinned thirty-four-year-old who had until recently worked at Heathrow Airport in the passenger security section. What he had loved most about his job was the power it gave him. He enjoyed shouting at people to put their laptop computers or other electronic devices in a separate tray and he especially liked finding things in bags that the passengers were not allowed to take through security, like a pair of scissors or a large bottle of water, because Jim had the authority to throw these items into the bin right before their eyes. Sometimes his job was to pat down people if he thought they might be hiding something in their clothes. Jim had a knack for picking the people who would hate it the most. An angry businessperson already late for a plane. A parent with a screaming baby. An old man who was already feeling humiliated by having to hold up his trousers because his belt had had to be removed. Jim would relish pulling his victims aside and treating them as if they were criminals.

Oh yes, Jim loved his job. He also loved the uniform,

and the routine, and the repetition. Even though he didn't care for his fellow workers, this was the first time in Jim's life he had found a place where he fitted in, and it made him happy to know he could do this for the rest of his life.

Then one day Jim's life plan was suddenly ruined by a mysterious eleven-year-old boy.

It all started when a fire broke out in the passenger scanning area.

For a few minutes there was pandemonium, and though a great deal of equipment was damaged by the flames, there were no casualties. None of the airport staff knew what had started the fire, but checking the footage later on the CCTV, Jim discovered what appeared to be a single frame of a boy diving through the body scanner a split second before the fire broke out.

Jim had no idea who this boy on the screen was, but he was convinced he was somehow connected with the incident.

Unfortunately, none of Jim's colleagues believed him. Jim absolutely hated it when he wasn't taken seriously, so he had shown the video to his bosses. After much squinting at the screen, Jim's bosses put it down to a glitch in the video system. 'Anyway, little boys don't just appear out of thin air,' they said.

When Jim had got angry with them for not taking him seriously, they chuckled and told him to calm down. Big mistake. Jim felt ashamed, and shame is the red chilli pepper of emotions.

Jim carried his sizzling-hot shame home with him and logged on to the internet. If his bosses weren't going to listen to him, then maybe someone on the internet would. He posted the picture of the mysterious boy flying through the air on Twitter and Facebook.

And guess what? It worked.

Within a few hours the photo was featured on a dozen blogs devoted to conspiracy theories such as 'Is Bigfoot real?' and 'Are our mobile phones listening to everything we say?' The picture was even picked up by an online news website.

Jim came to work that day feeling triumphant, but before he had even put on his uniform, he was called into the boss's office and fired.

Jim had broken the rules by taking airport security images home with him and then sharing them online.

Just like that, Jim Tindle had not just lost the job he loved, he had also lost his place in the world. In the days that followed, Jim couldn't bear to speak to or even see another person, and so he stayed inside his little flat with the curtains drawn with only his laptop for company . . . and then something wonderful happened.

It had been while scrolling through the online news that Jim saw Nelson. He was in a photo of a family gathered around a teenage girl called Celeste who had just been found alive after a kidnapping incident in South America.

Jim whooped with joy. The mysterious boy he had

seen on the tape was real. His name was Nelson Green and he was even wearing the same hooded top from the blurry video.

Jim was sure it was no coincidence, but this time he decided to keep his findings to himself until he could prove without doubt that he had been right all along.

Without a job, Jim wasn't able to afford the rent on his flat so he moved into his white van. He didn't care. He had enough money for petrol and Jaffa Cakes, and even more importantly, he had a new sense of purpose: to find Nelson Green and prove he started the fire that cost Jim his job.

It took most of the summer for Jim to locate Nelson and his family, and for a few days he parked himself across the street from their home. Like a private investigator, Jim made notes about everything he observed Nelson doing that summer: all of the boy's late-night trips to the park and London Zoo. From an oak tree on the other side of the school fence, Jim had even observed the rugby game during which Nelson appeared to fly for a moment, and it was while following Nelson and his sister one night that he had discovered the bike workshop. While crouched outside it, Jim heard Nelson talk of Uncle Pogo, Doody, something called a 'sin extractor' and the names of seven invisible creatures that had been extracted from Nelson's soul: Nosh, Spike, Stan, Puff, Hoot, Crush and Miscr.

Jim had been too excited to sleep for the previous few nights. He lay awake in his van imagining how terrific it was going to feel when he not only proved to the folks at work that he had been right all along, but that he had also uncovered a story the likes of which had never been heard before. The story would probably make him rich, he would certainly be famous, and best of all, he would be taken seriously and the red-hot shame that kept bubbling up when he thought about being fired would finally be cooled.

Now you know who Jim Tindle is.

But Nelson and his monsters were only just about to find out . . .

THERE WAS A KNOCK
AT THE DOOR

The monsters froze. Nelson's heart raced.

'Ivan?' said Nelson. 'Is that you?'

The door opened, and there stood Jim Tindle, a creepy wide smile on his pale, narrow face. What made the expression creepy was that his eyes did not join in with the smile. They remained emotionless, almost blank. Recognizing Jim from the van, Nelson backed away from the door and tripped over Crush.

'It's all right; I'm not gonna hurt you, Nelson,' said Jim with a fake little laugh.

'Do you know this bloke?' whispered Spike. The other monsters tensed and hissed and growled, like animals readying to attack their prey.

Nelson held up his hand, a sign that told his monsters to wait.

'Who are you?' said Nelson. 'And how do you know my name?'

'I'm Jim. You don't know me. But I know all about you. The fire you started at the airport. And your little invisible friends.'

'What do you mean?' said Nelson, starting to feel very sick.

'I've been following you for ages now. I know everything. I just need you to admit it all on camera, and I swear I will never bother you again.'

There was a pause. Jim was waiting for Nelson to reply, but Nelson was too shocked by what he had just heard to speak. The idea that he had been followed, and that his monsters were not a secret any more, chilled him to the bone.

'Can I kill him?' snarled Stan.

'No you can't!' shouted Nelson.

'Are you talking to them? They're all here now, aren't they? Spike, Nosh, Stan . . .' Jim enjoyed seeing the colour drain out of Nelson's face as he listed the names.

'See? I know all about you and these creatures you've got I heard you talking about the sin extractor and how it works . . .' Jim took his phone out of his pocket and switched on the video mode.

'Please. For your own sake. You've got to go away and leave us alone,' said Nelson in a shaky voice.

'Oh, I will, after you just do this one thing for me. I promise. Now, just start by saying your name into the camera.'

Nelson knew exactly what Stan was going to do if he didn't get his own fear under control.

'Let's start from the beginning,' urged Jim. 'Your name is Nelson Green, isn't that right?'

SMACK!

The phone flew out of Jim's hand and hit the ceiling of the workshop. Before it had even landed on the ground, Jim was flying backwards out of the door, barrelled along by Stan, who roared like a tiny lion.

'Aaaaaargh!' cried Jim.

It was the last sound he made before a cloud of stinky purple gas rendered him unconscious.

THE MAGNIFICENT LADY OF KNIGHTSBRIDGE

Mrs Ailsa Linley was tiny, and almost a hundred years old, but she swished through the streets of Knightsbridge, London, as if she were on the red carpet leading to her very own premiere. Wearing her late husband's tuxedo, slippers on her feet, a cigarette in one hand and her loyal Alsatian, Max, trotting by her side on a leash, she was the very definition of magnificent. It was a shame no one was around to see Ailsa, but she much preferred to take her morning walk before the tourists swarmed the streets.

Though people often found Max intimidating, he was a quiet and gentle soul, which is why Ailsa was startled to hear him bark suddenly.

'What are you barking at, Maxy? Huh? What is it, darling?'

They had stopped in front of the famous luxury department store called Harrods, and Max had jumped up at one of the display windows, his front paws pressed against the glass, his bark painfully loud.

'You silly dog. It's just a mannequin.' Ailsa tugged at Max's leash, but for the first time in his life, Max did not obey. His barking became more aggressive.

'Maxy! Stop it! Look. See? It's not a real man, it's just a . . .' Ailsa didn't finish her sentence because she realized she was wrong and Max was right. There was a real man lying fast asleep in the window display. He was tucked up under a polka-dot duvet, a baby's dummy in his mouth, and a shower cap on his head. He was surrounded by cuddly toys.

'Darling Maxy, you're quite right. There seems to be a fellow asleep in the window. At least, I *think* he's asleep. How very odd.' Rather than alert anyone then and there, Ailsa finished her usual walk around the park, came home, gave Max his breakfast, washed her face, applied very thick moisturizer to her face and hands, made a pot of coffee, lit a cigarette, and settled into her reading chair by the window. Only then did she call the police. The nice thing about this chair, other than it being the most comfortable chair in the world, was that it gave her a view of the street below, where, soon after making her call, she watched police cars arrive and escort the pale mystery man from Harrods.

Then, with Max curled around her feet and the morning sun creeping across her carpet, Ailsa Linley took her nap.

THE LAUGHTER THAT MADE A CARTON OF MILK EXPLODE

No one had ever heard Stan whistle before, but since he and the other monsters had stuck Jim in the window of Harrods he had not stopped whistling 'Singin' in the Rain'. He was even whistling it as they all walked behind Celeste and Nelson on their way to school.

'What did they do with that van man?' asked Celeste.

'Well?' said Nelson, turning round to face his monsters. Stan had refused to tell Nelson what they had done for fear of making him angry with them.

'Answer Cel's question. What did you lot do with that man?' The monsters all appeared to be pleased with themselves, which made Nelson uneasy.

'Put it this way. He ain't gonna be givin' us any more hassle and you can cross me off the wish list cos I've 'ad mine now,' said Stan with a wicked chuckle.

'You didn't hurt him, did you?'

'Oh, do let's tell Nelson! It was such fun!' Hoot was giddy with excitement.

'This is not making me feel any better.'

'Master Nelson,' mumbled Miser. 'We did not harm him in any way. Stan simply made certain that Jim Tindle never bothers you or us again. Ever.'

At this, all of the monsters exploded with laughter. Though Celeste couldn't hear it, the sound made Nelson clutch his ears. Any bird within earshot took to the sky. Worms wriggled deeper into the soil. Cats shivered. Dogs howled. A carton of milk exploded in a kitchen across the street.

When the monsters had finally pulled themselves together, Nelson sighed and turned to his sister. They were opposite Nelson's school.

'What did they say?' asked Celeste.

'Just that we won't be bothered by that man any more and that we don't need to worry.'

'Do you trust them?' said Celeste. 'Seriously? Because if there's even a tiny chance this man could come back again, we need to tell the police right now.'

'I trust them,' said Nelson, and Crush let out a triumphant 'HONK!'

'OK, well let's hope that's the end of it. Go on then, Nelse. Have a good day and I'll see you back at home later.' Celeste turned to face the monsters she could not see but knew were close by. 'And you lot, stay out of trouble, please.'

'We will!'

'Bye, Celeste!'

'We love you!'

'See ya later!'

'Toodle-doo!'

'Baa-bye!'

'Hoooonk!'

Though they also knew she couldn't hear them, the monsters waved and called out their goodbyes anyway.

Celeste climbed on to her bike and cycled away as Nelson crossed the street to school, leaving his monsters behind.

'Don't be all worry-worry, Nelly-son! Iz all gonna be good now dat man gone!' Nosh called as Nelson passed through the school gates.

'It's not gonna be good, though, is it?' moaned Spike. 'I'm the last one on the list. Once I've had my wish, we have to leave him forever.'

'Yeah, well, you don't even know what you want, so we could be here forever at this rate,' said Stan.

'Actually,' replied Spike. 'I know what I want to do now. And I want to do it tonight.'

IF U EVA COM BAK
WE WIL DISTROY U

'His name is James Marcus Tindle, thirty-four years old, single. Currently living out of his van, which was towed away from East London last night. A pretty ordinary bloke, and we're not sure what drove him to break into Harrods just to take a nap.'

The police officer looked up from her notebook to see her chief inspector with tears in her eyes and the final Harry Potter book in her hands.

'Uh . . . you all right, Chief Inspector?'

'Sorry, I'm on the last few chapters. He's about to face Voldemort. But . . . uh, I'll come back to this . . .' Realizing this was neither the time nor the place to discuss Harry Potter, she slipped her bus ticket between the pages as a bookmark, took a deep breath and returned to the matter at hand. 'Right then. This man in Harrods. What do we know about him?'

'No previous convictions, no driving offences or anything. A few months back he was fired from his job at Heathrow Airport for a minor breach of regulations. No wife or kids. Parents are next of kin. Dad lives alone in Scotland; Mum remarried and lives in Essex. Ambulance team gave him the once-over. Said apart from signs of exhaustion, he's perfectly healthy. The only trouble is, he says he has no memory of how he got there. It's like he may have had a blackout or something.'

'Hmm. How did he get in?'

'That's the one thing we're not completely sure of. The only sign of a break-in was a door on the roof that had been broken in half.'

'The *roof* of Harrods?'

'Yes, but there was no way of him getting up there without a fire-engine ladder. Even weirder was that he didn't show up on any CCTV footage. It's like he just appeared in the window.'

'Well, it's obvious he must have stayed in the shop after it closed and hidden somewhere.'

'I suppose so. I mean, yes, you're right.'

The chief inspector was fast losing interest in Jim Tindle and beginning to feel Harry Potter calling her back to the story.

'Look, this Jim Tindle is probably just a loner after a bit of attention. His photo's all over the news today. So just give him a warning and maybe keep an eye on him for a bit, but otherwise I think we're done with this bloke.'

The police officer nodded. 'Yes.'

She hadn't even left the room before the chief inspector was back at Hogwarts.

The Central Line train to Epping roared into the station,

screeched to a halt, sucked up hundreds of people and wailed as it disappeared into the tunnel.

A pregnant lady called Chloe was standing by a seat reserved for people like her, but it was occupied by a man. Normally Chloe would have no problem in asking for the seat, but there was something about the man's eyes and the way he was twitching and rubbing his arm that made her feel uneasy, so she clung to the rail and turned to look away from him.

Jim Tindle didn't even notice the pregnant woman standing right in front of him. He pushed back the sleeve of his jacket as far as it would go to reveal a message written on his skin in black pen.

IF U EVA COM BAK WE WIL DISTROY U

He knew the message had been written by the monsters. (He was right. It had been written by Stan, who wasn't very good when it came to spelling.) And though he could not remember them putting him in Harrods, he knew they were responsible. He licked his thumb and tried to rub the ink away. Of course, they had used a permanent marker. It would take weeks before their message would start to fade. Even so, he rubbed the letters so hard that his skin began to turn red.

The train suddenly stopped. They had reached the next station. Jim yanked his sleeve back down and looked up just in time to see his fellow passengers turn away from him. One of them was reading a newspaper with a photo of Jim asleep in the window of Harrods on the front page.

Shame and anger pulled his stomach into a fierce little knot. Everyone in the carriage knew who he was. The doors were already closing when Jim leaped from his seat, pushed past Chloe, and sat down in one of the metal seats on the platform. Fluttering by his feet was another newspaper. Jim snatched it up and stared at the image of himself asleep in the shop window, a baby's dummy in his mouth. The headline read:

NUT TAKES NAP IN HARRODS

He shuddered. He could never go back to Nelson now. There was no way he could risk whatever those monsters might do to him next time. His mission to expose them to the world was over, Jim realized, grinding his teeth in frustration.

He had to go back to his ordinary life and try to forget about it. The problem now was that the chances of finding another job this side of Christmas were practically zero. He was now the famous 'nut' who slept in Harrods. New employers need only google his name and this image would appear. Who could trust a man who did something like that? He only had £25 and some loose change in his pocket, which wasn't nearly enough money to get his van out of the police compound.

Jim had nowhere to go and no one to turn to.

And it was at this low moment, the lowest moment of his already low-flying life, that Jim suddenly saw the light. Well, it wasn't really a light; it was a poster. But it had the same effect on Jim as a lighthouse to a ship lost in a storm. Plastered to the wall on the other side of the platform was a poster for the latest exhibition at the Museum of London: 'Wren's Inventions'. As well as a photo of Doody and Pogo, whom Jim recognized from the telly, the poster showed a few examples of Sir Christopher Wren's inventions, and among them was an image of the sin extractor. Jim had seen it on TV and heard Nelson talking about it. He knew this was the device used to create the invisible monsters. Why had no one else tested it?

The tracks began to crackle. The next train was about to arrive. Jim felt the satisfying *click* of an idea falling into place. He stood up and dropped the newspaper on the floor. Wind as warm as breath rushed through the platform and blew the paper away.

If he couldn't get Nelson to admit he had monsters, then maybe he, Jim Tindle, could make some monsters of his own. He wasn't at all sure how to do it or if it would even work, but he had nothing to lose in trying.

'STAND CLEAR OF THE CLOSING DOORS,' warned a voice coming from the loudspeakers.

And a few noisy seconds later, the train and Jim Tindle had gone.

GOODNIGHT, NELSON

'I wish we didn't have to do rehearsals on a Saturday. Honestly, Katy Newman is nightmare,' said Nelson to his monsters as he crawled into his tent, which was still at the end of his garden. He was shivering and wet from the rain, which was pounding noisily on the roof of the tent. 'She made us sing those songs from *Bugsy Malone* a billion times. She keeps going on about us having to be perfect, like we're in a real West End show or something. Now I will never get those songs out of my head.'

Nelson started to hum 'You Give a Little Love' as he wiped his wet hair back from his forehead and looked around at his monsters. They all looked glum, and they had every reason to be.

'Why did you all want to meet here instead of the workshop? You know it's safer there.'

Crush honked and cuddled up next to Nelson.

'All right, I know how you're all feeling,' said Nelson. 'Spike's is the last wish. But it's not fair to be sad about that now. We can't ruin whatever Spike wants to do just because he's the last one.'

'Let's just get on wiv it,' Stan growled.

'So have you made up your mind, Spike?'

Spike nodded without looking up at Nelson.

'Well? What do you want to do?'

Instead of replying, Spike covered his mouth and nose. The other monsters did the same. Crush pressed his trumpet-like mouth into the sleeping bag.

Nelson was about to say 'What are you all doing?' but he only got as far as 'What . . .' when a cloud of purple gas engulfed him, his eyelids drooped, and his body slumped forward to the ground.

Without a word to each other, the monsters rushed out of the tent to let the gas disperse. The rain fell on them so hard you couldn't separate the rain drops from their tears.

'It's safe . . . to go . . . back in,' said Puff miserably. For the first time in days he wasn't floating.

The other monsters crawled back into the tent, and together they tucked Nelson into his sleeping bag. Crush stroked the wet hair on his forehead and cooed like a wood pigeon.

'We shouldn't 'ave done it like diss,' stammered Nosh.

'Course we should,' snapped Stan. 'Anyway, it was Spike's wish.'

They all looked at Spike, who had tears rolling down his green cheeks.

'All I wanted was to not have to say goodbye to him,' he said with a sniff. 'Can you imagine how *hideous* it would be to see him say goodbye to us? I don't ever want to feel what that's like. That's my wish.'

'Yeah, well, ya got ya wish. Now let's get on wiv it,' said Stan, his eyes glistening.

Miser picked up the fluffy toy pigeon, inside which the needle from the sin extractor was hidden.

'Aw, Nelly-son. Me gonna miss you so much,' said Nosh, his voice cracking, his bottom lip wobbling.

'At least . . . we'll all be together . . . mixed together . . . in his soul . . . like before we were born,' Puff said as he crawled up beside Nelson.

'Hooooooonk,' wailed Crush, still stroking Nelson's hair.

'Oh, lemme just look at Nelly-son a lickle bit more before we goin',' said Nosh longingly.

Miser nodded, and the monsters gathered closely around their beloved Nelson to watch him sleep for one more minute, while just a few miles away, Jim Tindle entered the Museum of London.

JIM AT THE MUSEUM

Jim's heart thumped in his chest, partly due to having drunk a can of energy drink, but mainly because a security guard had just entered the staff toilets where Jim was hiding.

'Anyone still in here?' barked the guard, and though of course Jim did not reply, the guard was not completely satisfied that the room was empty. First, he stooped to look under the doors. No feet could be seen. Jim was crouched on top of the toilet seat. Then the guard stood up and pushed open the cubicle doors, one after the other. Jim cursed himself for not locking his cubicle door, and then braced himself to be revealed as it swung open.

But the security guard did not see Jim. He was too busy looking at his reflection in the mirror on an adjacent wall. Until that morning, the security guard had had a formidable beard, but his new girlfriend had insisted he shave it off. Now he regretted it like mad. The guard stepped closer to the mirror, rubbed his newly smooth chin and realized he had liked his beard more than he liked his new girlfriend. Angry with himself, the guard growled as he switched out the lights and left the toilets.

Jim could not believe his luck. He had unwittingly been saved by a woman who didn't like beards.

With enormous relief and excitement, Jim realized the museum was entirely his now, though he was only interested in one exhibit. And within minutes he'd found it. Residing alongside a broken office chair, a water cooler and life-size cut-outs of Uncle Pogo and Doody was the sin extractor. Jim had assumed getting access to it would be tricky, but an 'incident' surrounding the sin extractor a few days earlier had meant that it was being stored temporarily in a corridor right next to the staff toilets. Jim had no idea he had the monsters to thank for making his plan so much easier.

Jim removed the sheet of cardboard that had been placed over the device and gently lowered his right palm over the needles. He expected to find them as dull as old nails and was shocked to discover how fiercely sharp they were. Not only that, but, like a magnet, he could feel his hand being drawn to them.

Crouching beside the extractor, Jim reached underneath and picked up one of the copper test tubes held in the iron rack. It was inscribed with the word 'ENVY'.

'One of the deadly sins,' said Jim, remembering what he'd seen on Doody's documentary. He poked his finger inside, to find it dirty and empty, before replacing it in the rack with the others.

Jim stood up a little too quickly and was struck by a flash of dizziness. He grabbed the side of the sin extractor to steady himself, and its 350-year-old joints creaked under his weight. The cut-outs of Doody and Pogo watched as Jim took off his green army surplus jacket and dropped it on the floor. Next he took off his navy-blue knitted sweater, and then his black T-shirt. Glancing over his shoulder to make sure he was in alignment with the table, Jim took a deep breath and began slowly lowering himself backwards as if into a very hot bath. As his elbows were about to touch the edges of the table, Jim suddenly slipped and dropped heavily on to the needles with a horrid *squelch*. The pain was so sharp and so intense that Jim was paralysed. He couldn't even move the air from his lungs to scream. It was pure blazing agony.

And then suddenly it wasn't.

The agony was replaced by a rush of bliss. Tears of happiness sprang from Jim's closed eyes and he groaned in ecstasy. He could not remember ever feeling so warm and safe, and when he opened his eyes he was no longer inside the Museum of London but lying in his father's arms.

THE ARM THAT BROKE
AND THE DAD WHO CARED

It was an afternoon in spring. Jim was four years old and sitting on his father's lap in the back of a taxi. Jim had fallen off a climbing frame in the park and broken his arm, and his father had rushed him to hospital. In the memory, Jim couldn't feel any pain in his arm, only his father gently stroking his forehead. 'You're going to be all right, Jimmy. What a brave boy you are. Yes, you are. So brave. You know I love you, don't you, son? I love you very much.' The feeling of being in his father's arms, of being loved so much by him, had filled Jim's entire being with the purest, richest form of happiness a human can feel. And suddenly the memory was over, and pain sent Jim twisting off the sin extractor and on to the floor.

As Jim huddled there, breathless, cold and disorientated, he thought he could still smell his father's cologne. In that moment, Jim did not think of Nelson Green, of revenge, or even of creating his own monsters. All he wanted was to return to the warmth and joy of his memories. Jim didn't even notice the steam rising from the seven copper test tubes that had toppled from the iron rack beneath the sin extractor, and though his back was covered in hundreds of tiny red dots of blood, Jim lowered himself on to the needles once again.

The shocking and paralysing pain returned, swiftly followed by the rush of bliss as another happy memory engulfed him. This time he was eight years old, lying on the carpet under the Christmas tree and looking up through the branches at the lights and baubles.

While Jim was immersed in this sumptuous memory, vapour and steam leaked out from underneath the sin extractor, but this time the copper test tubes were not in place to catch it. Whatever was being extracted from Jim was pouring on to the floor and collecting in silvery puddles that hissed and bubbled as if the floor were hotter than hell.

GOODBYE, NELSON

Miser laid the pen down and read the note he had just written.

'Mmmm. I think this should explain everything to Master Nelson.' He folded the paper in half and tucked it into the sleeping bag next to Nelson.

'Should we all hold hands, then?' said Hoot.

'I'm not holding hands with you,' grumbled Stan.

'Good idea, Hoot,' said Puff. 'All hold hands.'

With lightning speed, Miser whipped the sin-extractor needle out of the cuddly pigeon and jammed it into the middle of Nelson's chest. Nelson didn't even flinch. He was still fast asleep. No sooner had the needle pierced Nelson's skin than Miser felt that overwhelming pulling sensation.

'Hold tight! We can't leave anyone behind!' shouted Miser as his hand began to shrink and disappear into the needle he was holding on to. All of the monsters could feel the pull of the needle travelling through them.

'On second thoughts, I don't want to leave! I want to stay! I very, very much want to stay!' cried Hoot as he watched Miser's entire body shrink and funnel into the tip of the needle, like a sand timer in reverse.

'Too late! Hold on!' shouted Spike over the loud *whoosh*ing sound. Nelson's body shook beneath the sleeping bag like an astronaut during re-entry as, next into the needle, went Spike. His rubbery green body followed his stringy right arm into the tip of the needle, and with a *whoosh!* he was gone.

'Aaaah!' wailed Hoot, and though he tried to pull back, his yellow wing could not fight the powerful pull of the needle. 'Goodbye, my friends!' were his last words before he vanished, pulling Puff in behind him. The process of being returned to Nelson's soul suddenly sped up. Now that Hoot's reluctance to leave had been overcome, the others flowed as quickly as river water into the needle. Crush was the last in the chain and with one last 'HONK!' he vanished.

The *whoosh*ing stopped. The needle twitched in Nelson's chest. All was quiet except for Nelson's slow and gentle breaths.

And that was that.

Miser, Hoot, Puff, Nosh, Spike, Stan and Crush had returned to Nelson's soul.

HAPPINESS

While Jim had been lying steeped in happy moments from his past, the sin extractor he lay upon had been hissing and shaking. Seven types of monster were being extracted from his soul, their essence spilling out on to the museum floor, where they began to slither and take form. One was cactus-like; another was red and horned. There was a fluffy purple one, a chubby pink one, a slippery blue one, a yellow feathered one, and a trumpet-faced orange one. Each new monster bore a resemblance to Nelson's monsters but for three significant differences: they grew much bigger, each one reaching approximately five feet in height; their colours were duller and more dreary; and lastly, they were much, much, *much* uglier. They had lumps and bumps and warts and tufts of hair and lopsided faces with eyes that looked in different directions. Some were extremely skinny, some bloated as if about to pop, and some looked like they were made of melting wax.

The terrible thing was that this was the eighth time Jim had lain on the sin extractor. This meant there were now eight of each type of monster. Fifty-six monsters in total. With each new extraction, their ugliness had grown more profound and sickening.

None of them said a word. They simply stood in the darkness around their maker, breathing and panting and watching with wide eyes as Jim lay smiling on the sin extractor.

They could feel the happiness he was experiencing and they liked it. They wanted to keep this feeling as much as he did, so when Jim fell to the floor feeling cold and sick, they felt it too, and eight trumpet-nosed monsters ran forward to pick him up.

'Honk! Honk! Honk!' they honked in raspy unison.

Jim looked up, his face covered in sweat, to see the monsters leaning down to help him.

'Once more,' whispered Jim, and the monsters obliged by lifting Jim off the floor and laying him back on the extractor.

MIXED FEELINGS

Nelson knew something was different before he had even opened his eyes. His body felt heavy and uncooperative, and when he yawned it felt as if his lips were swollen. When he finally managed to heave his eyelids open and sit up, he realized it was morning, and he was alone.

'Guys?' Nelson's voice croaked. 'Stan? Puff? Spike? . . . Aaah!'

Nelson looked down to see the sin-extractor needle sticking out of his chest. He was almost sick at the sight of it and it took him several deep breaths before he could summon the courage to pull the needle out. Though it was buried an inch into his chest, it didn't hurt a bit once it was out.

Nelson looked at the needle and understood what had happened. His friends were gone for good. Without warning, he felt the urge to sneeze.

'Honk!'

Nelson sat up straight. Did he just make a honking sound? It certainly didn't sound like his usual sneeze. He rubbed his nose. It felt normal. He must have been mistaken.

Nelson laid the needle beside him and unzipped his sleeping bag, to find a large piece of white paper tucked inside. He turned the paper over, and written in purple felt tip was the following message.

Master Nelson,
If you are reading this it means we have successfully been reabsorbed into your soul. It was Spike's wish to leave as we did. He did not want to say goodbye. We are sorry to have used Puff to put you to sleep but we felt it was for the best.
Goodbye,
Miser, Hoot, Spike, Crush, Stan, Puff and Nosh
XXXXXXX
PS: We hope you do not experience any side effects. We are not 100 % sure what the outcome will be.

'That's it? That's *all* they wrote?' said Nelson in disbelief to an empty tent. 'Wow. After all this time, after everything we've been through . . . just a stupid little note?'

Nelson felt a rush of anger, and kicked out so hard that his foot tore through the bottom of the sleeping bag.

Nelson sighed, and touched the back of his hair where it met his neck. He had half expected it to grow all at once, but it felt the same as it always did. 'Urgh. Nothing's even changed. I'm still the same.'

It was the day of his uncle's wedding, but the thought of it made Nelson want to go back to sleep.

The *twang, twang, twang* sound of trampoline springs meant that his neighbour George was already bouncing in his back garden. Nelson unzipped the tent and, sure enough, there was George bouncing up and down behind the garden wall.

'All right, George?' said Nelson dully, and for the first time in ages, George spoke.

'You slept in a tent.'

Nelson was caught by surprise to hear George respond. 'Uh, yeah, I did sleep in a tent.'

'I did that once. In Scouts. I slept in a tent. It was cold, though.'

'I didn't know you were in the Scouts.'

'I'm not any more.'

'Oh.'

Remember, George is still bouncing up and down while this conversation is taking place.

'They said I had to leave because I didn't join in enough.'

'Right. Joining in's probably a big deal in Scouts.'

'Yeah. It is. And badges. Badges are a huge deal.'

'Badges, yeah.'

The conversation suddenly reached a dead end, and for a moment neither of them could think of how to keep it going. George kept bouncing, and Nelson thought that maybe it was best to make his excuses and be on his way, when George came up with a conversation kick-starter.

'The wedding's today, isn't it?'

Nelson was impressed by what a good spy George was.

'Actually, yeah, it is.'

'Your uncle is getting married to the history man off the telly.'

'Doody.'

'It was on the news.'

'Was it?'

'I've never been to a grown-up party.'

Nelson realized why George was being so chatty. He wanted to come to the wedding party!

'Should be fun. The wedding's going to be at St Paul's Cathedral.'

'I went on a trip to St Paul's once. I did a brass rubbing of a saint. He had a thin face and he looked sad and he was carrying a goat. Or a weasel. It wasn't a very good rubbing.' George stopped bouncing and the silence that followed was massive.

Luckily for Nelson, Celeste chose that moment to push the back door open with her foot, carrying two cups of tea.

'I was just coming to wake you,' said Celeste. 'Oh, hello, George. You're up early.'

George snapped back to his usual silent and awkward self and resumed bouncing.

'So they really are gone,' said Celeste as she put down

Miser's letter on the kitchen table.

Nelson nodded while devouring a slice of toast and lowering another slice of bread into the toaster. 'I'm just gonna have one more. With peanut butter this time. And jam.'

'You all right?'

Nelson shrugged. 'Hungry. Really hungry.'

'I mean, you don't have to pretend with me, Nelson. It's natural to feel upset.'

'I know – I just . . . I don't know how I feel. I mean, I'm hungry. And tired.'

'Maybe you just need time to, you know, process it.'

'I CAN'T BELIEVE THEY WOULD JUST LEAVE WITHOUT SAYING GOODBYE!' roared Nelson, and he kicked the kitchen cupboards.

Minty shot out of her basket and began barking at Nelson.

'Whoa! Nelse! Where did that come from?!' Celeste jumped up from her chair and grabbed her brother's shoulders to steady him. Nelson was shaking and looked as surprised by his own outburst as Celeste did. Minty continued to bark angrily at Nelson.

'Quiet, Minty! Shh! Stop it! Oh, I'm sorry, Cel,' said Nelson breathlessly. 'I didn't mean to get angry, I just . . . I just want some more toast.'

He didn't wait for the timer to finish and instead ejected the toast and covered it in jam and peanut butter with all the urgency of someone whose life depended on toast.

'OK, I think you just need to take things easy at the wedding today, Nelse. Here, have some tea,' said Celeste, pulling out a chair for him.

Nelson was still shaking when he sat down. Minty finally gave up the angry barking and collapsed back in her bed.

'Yeah. Yeah, you're right. Sorry. I do feel a bit weird.' Nelson took a sip of tea. She'd added extra sugar, which was just what he needed. He heard the hiss of the shower running upstairs. This meant he had only ten more peaceful minutes before his mother appeared wrapped in towels and barking wedding-related orders. The need to sneeze came over him once again.

'Honk!'

Celeste laughed, thinking Nelson had made the noise as a joke. But he hadn't. It had just burst out of him.

'Well, I've got to be honest, your monsters were great and everything, but it'll be nice for things to be normal again, don't you think?'

Nelson nodded, but neither of them had any clue that things were about to get as far from normal as they could possibly be.

TINDLE'S UGLY ARMY

A tremendous fire tore its way through the Museum of London. Alarm bells rang and water poured from ceiling-mounted fire extinguishers, but they were powerless against the great flames furiously turning priceless historical artefacts into ash. Jim Tindle's pink and greedy monsters were responsible. Like Nosh, they had incinerated what they ate. The flames leaped from the holes in their head and within seconds the ceiling had caught on fire. Maybe if there had only been a few greedy monsters there would not have been so much damage, but now there were twenty-three of them.

Let's do the maths. If Jim Tindle had twenty-three Greed monsters, this meant he had performed twenty-three sin extractions, and if seven monsters were made each time, that meant he had created a grand total of 161 monsters.

That is a lot of monsters.

If it were not for the fire, Jim would have continued to plunge back into happy memories, but now he was forced to flee the building. He was drained of energy, he could barely walk, and the smoke from the fire had turned his sweaty skin black. The monster army lifted him and carried him above their heads like the star striker of a football team. When it seemed as if they had reached a dead end, twenty-three red and very angry monsters with horns twisting out of their heads smashed their great fists  through the walls, and they all poured out of the museum to safety.

A bus screeched to a halt as debris and smoke flew across the road. Sirens wailed in the distance as the emergency services headed towards the fire. The museum was closed today but tourists were always walking through this area, and now they were running as fast as they could away from the clouds of black smoke and falling ash. Everyone was too terrified to stop and look, or even film what was happening with their smartphones. They would not have seen the monsters, but they would have seen Jim floating about six feet above the ground, shirtless and blackened by smoke.

'I need it! We have to go back for it!' cried Jim suddenly. The monsters knew he was talking about the sin extractor.

'HONK!' wailed all of the Crush-like monsters in agreement. It was a deafening sound. Like a fleet of car ferries leaving port at once. In response to their honking command, the blue Miser-like monsters bowed, before running back into the burning building.

Jim couldn't help but laugh. Here he was, held aloft in the middle of the streets of London by his very own monster army. Though he craved the bliss of another happy memory, the power he now felt was divine.

The slippery blue monsters reappeared from the burning museum carrying the sin extractor between them. One of the monsters was on fire and collapsed in the road. A taxi drove straight into the wretched creature, and the driver ran from his car with no idea of what he had just hit.

Jim was unable to take his eyes off the burning monster thrashing around in the street and sending the taxi flying into a wall. How quickly he had adjusted to having a monster army! Twenty-four hours ago this idea would have seemed incomprehensible to him, but now it felt perfectly normal. In fact, it felt like it was all meant to be.

'Where should we go first?' asked Jim.

All of the monsters pointed north.

'REVENGE!' they roared, and once again Jim laughed at how exhilarating it was to be a leader. No one had ever seen the world from his point of view, and now an entire army of monsters felt exactly what he felt: a burning desire for revenge upon Nelson Green and the seven measly monsters who had ruined his life.

THE WEDDING OF DOODY AND POGO

They were only an hour into it, but already this was the greatest wedding party anyone had ever been to. It was the perfect combination of terrific music, wonderful food and drink, stunning location and, at the top of the list of essential ingredients, two lovely hosts. Doody and Pogo not only looked magnificent in their suits, but they radiated happiness. All the guests found themselves under Pogo and Doody's happy spell and were soon dancing with old friends in the crypt of St Paul's Cathedral. Christmas parties, book launches, even awards ceremonies had been held in the crypt, but never had it been decorated as beautifully as it was now. There were flowers, and plants, and even little trees everywhere. And I mean everywhere. Pogo loved plants as much as his father had done, and the crypt felt like a tropical jungle rather than the resting place of Admiral Nelson.

'Let's get a picture of us all together!' shouted Nelson's mum, and a group quickly swarmed together in front of her: Doody, Pogo, Nelson's dad, Celeste, Ivan and Nelson. 'I wanna nice smile from you, Nelse, not that ruddy frown you've been wearing all day,' she said with raised eyebrows, which meant this was not a discussion point.

Nelson attempted a smile.

'Here, take this of us all, will ya?' said Nelson's mum to the waiter serving drinks. He put down his tray and held her phone up to his eyeline.

'Everyone say "Bees Gees"!' shouted Doody.

'Bees Gees!' they all replied, and the waiter took the photo. Everyone rushed to see how it looked.

'Oh, that's the best photo ever!' squealed Nelson's mum. 'I mean, Nelse looks a bit washed out, but look at us all! Ha ha! This is going on the wall at home.'

Nelson only had a second to glance at the photo before his mum put the phone away, but it was enough time to see she was right. He did look washed out. It wasn't that he didn't enjoy being at the wedding; he just felt so strange today. Even when he had been summoned to present the wedding rings, Nelson had felt a burning desire to keep them in his pocket. Part of his brain was telling him to hand over the rings, while another wanted desperately to keep them. His hesitation was mistaken for nerves by Celeste, who helped him out. Once the rings were on his uncles' fingers, Nelson had felt an uncontrollable surge of love towards Pogo and Doody and ran forward to embrace them both. Everyone had laughed and thought it was a delightful moment, but Nelson had quickly retreated, feeling ashamed. And now, looking at the photo of himself, he wished he looked better. Handsome like Ivan.

'All right, folks! How we doing out there?' Doody had

leaped on to the stage and grabbed the microphone, his big toothy grin wider than ever before. Everyone turned and cheered.

'Fancy a bit o' line dancin' then?'

The guests cheered again.

'Well, give it up for Rodeo Jones and his Wild Horses!' Four musicians dressed for the Wild West took to the stage: a drummer, a violinist, a double bass player, and a singer with two large front teeth and a greased centre parting, who took hold of the mic.

'I'm Rodeo Jones and this here is my band, the Wild Horses!' It was without doubt the most unconvincing American accent anyone had ever heard. The band began to play an infectious country rhythm, and Rodeo Jones began to sing instructions to the guests while slapping his thigh.

'Get in line, get in line. Ladies left, fellas right. Step to the beat now, one, two, three . . .'

He may have had an awful American accent, but Rodeo Jones had an incredible power over the crowd. Within seconds he had divided the room into two rows of dancers who obeyed his every word.

'Face your partner! Right hand up! Take their hand and round ya go!'

It worked! Everyone was dancing perfectly together. Celeste and Ivan could not stop laughing as they spun around, and even Uncle Pogo with his false leg was able to swing Doody around in time with the music. There was a smile on every face except Nelson's. He had managed to dodge his mother, for she would have insisted he join in, and he hid in a corner by the food table. It wasn't that he didn't want to join in, he just couldn't. Everyone else was having so much fun, but he didn't know how he felt. One minute he was tired, the next he was angry, then he was hungry and eating everything he could get his hands on. Looking past his uncles on the stage he could see Admiral Nelson's tomb. This is where it had started for our Nelson: camping out in the crypt of St Paul's on the night of the storm. It was here, as he lay asleep in a tent constructed by his Uncle Pogo, that his monsters had been born.

Nelson found himself looking down at his reflection in an empty silver drinks tray. He didn't like the way he looked. He wanted to change his hair. His shirt collar was too big and made his neck look too thin. He bared his teeth and thought they looked crooked and embarrassing.

'What am I doing?' said Nelson out loud, though everyone else was too busy dancing to hear him. He had never in his life cared what he looked like, and now he saw his face as a collection of flaws and defects.

Grabbing a lemonade and scoffing a handful of salted peanuts, Nelson snuck out through the door and climbed the stairs leading to the ground-floor exit.

The sunshine caught him by surprise, but when Nelson put up his hand to shield his eyes, the sun shone straight through.

Not just through the gaps in his fingers. Right through his skin and bone, as if he were made of glass.

GEORGE OF THE TRAMPOLINE

George had stayed out in his garden all morning. He hated being in the house when his father was watching the horse racing. The sound of the TV commentators yelling stupid horse names, and the way his father got so excited that white spit would gather in the corners of his mouth, made George feel queasy, so instead he sat outside on his trampoline looking at his bare feet. For the last few days he had been trying to make his toes separate by themselves. His left foot was quite obliging, but for some reason the toes on his right foot required Jedi-like concentration to get them to even budge. 'How come you lot are so tricky?' asked George of his toes. He tried again, pursing his lips, scrunching his nose and narrowing his eyes, when suddenly the house next door exploded.

George covered his head with his hands and screamed, but he could not be heard over the thundering roar of bricks and cement and glass crashing into next door's garden.

'What have you done?!' cried George's dad as he ran out of the back door.

'I didn't do anything! Their house just fell down,' said

148

George weakly while pointing to the remains of Nelson's home. It reminded George of the doll's houses he had seen at the Museum of Childhood. Those old Victorian toys were often displayed without their fronts so that you could see all the rooms on different levels inside, and it was the same for Nelson's house. George could clearly see the kitchen and the living room, while upstairs half of the bathroom was still there, as well as the landing area and a bit of the bedroom on the other side. Minty the dog ran out of the remains of the kitchen, covered in dust, and began barking angrily back at the house for waking her up.

'Good God, Jerry! What just happened?' George's mother had joined her husband in the garden.

'Look at that,' said George's father. 'Gas leak or something?'

'Oh! Lucky they were all out at the wedding. Call the police,' said George's mother and they both ran inside, leaving George on his trampoline. He could taste the dust in air. It was chalky, and it was weird to think that he was probably eating tiny particles that had once been a chair or a television, or even a toilet. George looked down at his feet and saw that a great deal of dust had collected in the dip he had made by sitting in the middle of the trampoline. He stood and brushed himself down, and when he looked back at the house he saw a bare-chested man smeared with black soot standing in what used to be his neighbours' upstairs bathroom.

George's mouth fell open. Seeing a house explode would be a pretty big surprise for anyone, but for some reason the sight of this stranger was even more shocking. He felt his heart race and his skin bristle with goosebumps. It was lucky for George that he could not see the army of hideous monsters that were also standing in the ruins of Nelson's house.

'Take me to that boy over there,' said the man angrily, and one of his yellow bird-like monsters crouched before him, allowing him to climb on its back.

George gasped at the sight of the stranger flying towards him, apparently unaided, but gasping made George's lungs fill with dust and he began to cough violently.

'Do you know where Nelson Green is?'

George was coughing too much to see the man talking to him, let alone answer him.

'Answer me! Do you know where Nelson Green is?' snapped the man.

George was still gasping for air when he looked up to see the man standing on his garden wall, glaring down at him.

'Wh-who are you?' stammered George.

'I asked you where Nelson Green is. So? Where is he? Do you know or not?' said Jim (because of course that's who it was), his anger rising with every word.

What George should have done was say he didn't know where Nelson was – or maybe even a shrug would have done it – but instead George made the mistake of saying, 'I'm not telling you.'

It was proof he knew exactly where Nelson was – and why one of Jim's cactus-shaped monsters stepped forward, plucked a needle from its own green flesh and jammed it right between George's eyes.

Don't worry, George didn't feel any pain. He was suddenly empty of all thought or self-awareness, which was good because he could now see the monsters and hear what they were saying, and if he had been conscious he might have died of fright.

'Now, tell our master where Nelson Green is,' hissed the horrible green monster, its veiny red eyes bulging so violently it looked as if they were about to fall out of their sockets.

Jim had never seen what his green monsters could do with their needles, and he watched, fascinated, as they extracted the truth from the little boy.

'He's gone to the wedding,' said George in a dreamy monotone voice.

'What wedding?' snapped the green monster.

'The wedding for the men who are getting married. I wanted to go too but I wasn't invi—'

'Just tell us where it is,' butted in the monster.

'I never get invited to parties. Ever since I did a wee on a bouncy castle at Jane Collins's birthday party.'

'Again! We do not care about any of this – just give us the location.'

'It wasn't my fault, I'd had loads of orange juice and—'

'Give me strength!' wailed the green monster. 'WHERE IS NELSON GREEN?' it screamed, and this time George seemed to shudder as if some trace of fear had found its way past the numbness of the needle sticking out of his head. There was a moment of silence as George swallowed before speaking.

'St Paul's Cathedral,' said George before the cactus needle was plucked from his head and he collapsed back on to the trampoline.

TRANSFORMER

Nelson felt his stomach lurch, and panic take hold, as he lowered his hand and saw that it was ghostlike. While the sleeve of his shirt remained solid, his hand was slowly fading away. He could still feel his fingers, but they were becoming translucent. The same thing was happening to his other hand.

Nelson looked around to see if anyone else had noticed. He was standing in a small garden area at the back of St Paul's, and through the iron fence he could see tourists walking by and taking pictures of the great dome.

I've gotta hide before anyone sees me, thought Nelson, and he crouched behind a small bush, took a deep breath, pushed up his sleeves and found he could see right through his arm to the bush behind.

'Oh no,' said Nelson out loud, but it wasn't his voice. It was deeper and raspier than usual. 'What's happening to me? What's happened to my voice?' He didn't sound like himself at all. In fact, he sounded like a monster. 'Side effects,' he growled, remembering the note his monsters had left him. 'I knew it. I knew something was wrong. Oh, those idiots! They haven't cured me of the curse; they've

made a total mess of me!'

Riiiiiiip! Nelson looked down at his shirt sleeves bursting open. His translucent arms were suddenly flooded with colour, ketchup red, and his hands ballooned into great puffy fists.

'Oh my God,' said Nelson in his new gravelly voice. 'Ow! Oww! OW!' he cried as a horn curled up and out of either side of his head, but no one could hear him or see him, even though people were everywhere. Like his monsters, Nelson was now not only invisible but also inaudible to normal human beings. The tourists walking by weren't reacting to him at all – they would only have been able to see his clothes, but even they were disappearing, ripped to shreds as his body transformed. Nelson grabbed his stomach and felt it bulge like a water-filled balloon over his legs. It was so heavy he fell forward on to the grass. His legs twitched behind him and, looking back, Nelson saw a wave of purple fur burst through his jeans and ripple right down to his ankles, where, instead of two feet, two purple paws popped through his sneakers and sprouted sharp yellow claws.

'Oooh nooo!' howled Nelson as he rolled on to his back

and covered his eyes with his great fists.

'OW!' he yelled, as pain shot through his fingers. He opened his eyes to see his chubby red hands now covered in cactus needles. 'Youchy!' He shook his hands and the needles flew away.

'What's happened to my face?' he croaked as he tentatively reached up to touch his cheeks. Needles pricked his fingers, and at once he recognized the feel of cactus flesh. The changes came quicker and quicker. His lips expanded, and a great purple tongue flopped out on to his green cheek. Nostrils that used to be so narrow now flared wide, sucking up air like two vacuum cleaners. His spine cracked and clicked and clacked as it grew longer to accommodate a new, taller body, while his ribs bowed and expanded and two more hands appeared from his sides, stretching away from his body on bendy orange arms. Something was pushing at his upper and lower back at the same time, and with such force that Nelson flipped on to his side. With a whip-like crack, a long, blue, rubbery tail shot out from the base of his spine, and at the end of the tail, little rubbery fingers flexed, while between his shoulder blades two little yellow wings unfurled. The transformation was complete and the pain stopped. Nelson didn't need a mirror to know exactly what he had become: a squished-up mega-mix of his seven monsters.

'Nightmare,' growled Nelson.

Nelson's clothes and shoes lay shredded all around him. He looked down at his purple paws and the claws slid out. They looked dangerously sharp.

'Well, Puff, I've got your legs and feet now,' said Nelson, as if Puff were right there. 'Don't tell me I have your farts too?'

The fists and the horns were certainly from Stan, and the orange arms from Crush. 'How am I doing this?' mumbled Nelson to himself as he made the little rubbery hand on the end of his blue tail wave. He couldn't understand how he was able to control all these new body parts that until a few seconds ago had never existed. Just thinking about the wings on his back made them flex and stretch as if ready for lift-off.

A great cheer came from inside the party, and Nelson looked back at the door, which was covered in an arch made of balloons. Back in the crypt, Doody and Pogo's guests were laughing and enjoying the food, while on the opposite side of the iron fence, tourists were gathering to tour the cathedral. No one could see the monster that was Nelson Green.

What to do next was a very big question. He needed help. Celeste! But she wouldn't be able to see him, so how . . . ? Maybe if he covered his hands in mud he could use sign language. But what would he say? 'Hey, Cel, look! I'm a monster now'? The realization that this might be how he would spend the rest of his life made him roar with anger.

'AAAAAAAARGH!' Tears rained from his eyes and ran down his prickly green cheeks. Those stupid monsters.

Why didn't they at least test their idea before trying it out on him? Now they were gone for good, and he would spend the rest of his life as a freaky cocktail of them all, invisible to everyone. He would be like a missing person. His mother would die of heartbreak, for sure. The whole point was to stop the curse, and now he was more cursed than ever before.

'AAAAAARGH!' he roared again, but no one heard except for the pigeons, who were terrified and flew away, never to return.

He felt shame and anger and sadness, but above all, Nelson felt hungry. The smell of onions coming from a food stall nearby was not just making his mouth water; it was making his stomach groan louder than a teenager who has been told to clean their room. Nelson licked his lips at the thought of eating a hamburger or five, and his tongue discovered a new set of teeth that were big, rough and full of gaps wide enough to fit a banana. A rumble as deep as an earthquake began to shake the bushes. Nelson pressed one of his four hands against his stomach, thinking that might be the cause of the tremor, but looking around, he could see the whole area was vibrating. The bus stop and the lamp posts shook as the sound grew louder and louder. Somewhere close by, a woman screamed, and Nelson looked up to see a sight even more strange and terrifying than his own transformed body: a great cloud of monsters flying down the street. Twenty-three of the bird-like creatures were carrying the rest of Jim's army beneath them, and when they reached the steps of St Paul's they dropped to the ground. No one in the street could see them, but everyone saw the cathedral doors being blown apart.

NELSON GREEN V.
THE UGLY ARMY

Tourists and tour guides and priests ran for their lives as what appeared to them to be invisible forces sent the pews flying in all directions. The only person who wasn't running anywhere was Jim Tindle, who was lowered to the ground by his flying monsters.

'That's where they are!' cried Jim, pointing at a doorway covered in an arch of balloons and roped off with a sign saying:

CRYPT CLOSED FOR PRIVATE EVENT

The wedding guests were in the midst of dancing to a country-and-western version of 'Kids in America', performed by Doody, Pogo and the wedding band, when an enormous blast knocked them all to the floor. Screams and cries and coughing could be heard in every part of the room as a dust cloud engulfed the crypt. The guests couldn't see each other – and they certainly couldn't see the monster army standing in the hole where the exit used to be.

Jim Tindle waited for the dust to settle before stepping inside.

'Quiet!' Jim shouted above the mayhem. 'I said quiet!' screeched Jim again, but no one could hear him over the panicked screams. 'Do something,' muttered Jim to his army. One of the largest of the red-horned monsters picked Jim up and held him above his head.

One by one, the party guests fell silent at the sight of Jim Tindle floating in mid-air.

'Finally,' said Jim. 'I thought you would never shut up.'

Pogo and Doody stood up together, their arms still linked from dancing.

'Who are heck are you?' shouted Doody angrily, and Pogo squeezed his arm fearfully. Jim ignored the question.

'I'm looking for Nelson Green.'

The room broke out into fearful whispers, and once again Jim became angry.

'SHUT UP!'

The crowd instantly did as they were told. Jim's greedy monsters were already walking among them, their rubbery blue arms snaking around the room while their little hands plucked wallets and jewellery from the unsuspecting guests.

'Please do not make me shout again. You will listen to me and you will answer my question, is that understood?'

Silence.

'IS THAT UNDERSTOOD?' yelled Jim Tindle, and every guest in the room cried 'Yes!'

Pogo and Doody were on the stage, peering over a speaker at Jim.

'Don't tell me this is one of your old boyfriends?' whispered Doody. Pogo shook his head to say this was no time for bad jokes.

'What was that?' whispered Pogo as something brushed past him. He had no idea it was the hand of a blue monster, searching his pockets for valuables. Pogo looked down at his false leg and saw the compartment in which he kept his mints pop open.

'Something just touched my leg.'

'Never mind that,' whispered Doody. 'Pogo, look. Look what's behind that floating bloke. What the heck is that doing here?'

Doody was pointing to the sin extractor. It was positioned just behind Jim, and though the metal legs were crooked and blackened from smoke, there was no mistaking the bed of needles. Doody and Pogo looked at each other in disbelief.

'I know he's here,' said Jim as his monster carried him in the air above the cowering guests.

Celeste scanned the dust and rubble for signs of her brother. Ivan was doing the same thing, while both her parents were still crouched on the floor.

'Now, for the last time,' said Jim, 'where is Nelson Green?'

'HOOOOOOONK!'

Jim spun around just in time to see monster Nelson

shooting forward on his yellow wings before snatching him out of the air. The guests only saw Jim Tindle screaming as he flew over their heads and straight up the staircase leading to the main hall.

'GET HIM!' roared Jim's monsters, and they chased Nelson through the party, knocking guests and rubble out of their way as they passed. Jim's sleepy purple monsters weaved slowly in and out of the panicked guests, letting off great clouds of purple sleeping gas. As the guests fell, one by one, into a deep sleep, Nelson gripped the greasy Jim Tindle so hard that Jim could barely breathe, flapping his wings and carrying them higher and higher until they were close to the top of the inside of the dome. Below, the visitors ran for the exit. No one could see the monsters, but everyone could see the terrifying destruction they were causing.

'What the heck are you?' wheezed Jim.

Nelson felt his lips shrink from a trumpet into a mouth shape, and words were formed.

'My monsters warned you. You should have stayed away from us.'

'Your monsters? I don't believe it . . . You're Nelson Green?'

'If I drop you, you're dead.'

'Oh my God, it is you! Well, you've changed in the last few days, eh!?' cried Jim with a giddy and sarcastic laugh. 'Still an annoying little git underneath it all, though!'

Nelson pulled Jim up close to his face with one of

his four hands. 'Why wouldn't you leave us alone?' he growled.

'All you had to do was admit to the truth! That you started that fire at Heathrow!' said Jim.

'We didn't start this.'

'I lost my job because of you!'

'You attacked my family and you've totally ruined my uncle's wedding,' said Nelson through large, gritted teeth. His anger was now so intense that it made his horns twist like corkscrews.

'And *you* ruined my life, so go ahead! Drop me! Go on! Whatever you do, it doesn't matter, cos I've got my own monster army and they are gonna kill you, Nelson Green!'

BLAM!

Nelson was hit right between the shoulder blades by one of Jim's bird monsters, and Jim fell from his grasp. A swarm of bird monsters caught him, and another attacked Nelson in mid-air, pecking and clawing at him as he fell towards the cathedral floor. It was like watching some very ugly eagles play with their food before they kill it.

Nelson's mighty red fists swelled and swiped the air, smashing beaks and sending feathers flying, before he landed on the edge of the Whispering Gallery with a tremendous *crash!* The stone barrier collapsed; Nelson had nothing to hold on to, and fell through the air and on to the cathedral floor. The pain of hitting the stone was so intense that his cry shattered all the stained-glass windows. And as the glass rained down on to the floor of the cathedral, Jim's monsters pounced on Nelson. Their combined weight was suffocating, and their blows and bites were blindingly painful. Nelson shook his head in an attempt to push the monsters off with his horns, but every time he knocked one monster away, another took its place.

Jim hugged his own chest. He was cold, and badly cut across the shoulders by Nelson's claws. He craved the happiness he felt from lying on the sin extractor, but that would have to wait until his monsters had killed Nelson Green, which by the looks of it would be fairly soon.

Nelson fought bravely and with tremendous strength, but he was no match for Jim's army. What they lacked in strength and ability, they more than made up for in numbers. No matter how hard Nelson kicked them, how fiercely he slapped them away, pummelled them with his fists, rammed them with his horns and throttled them with his tail, there was always another monster to take over.

It was beginning to feel less like a fight and more like slow suffocation. Nelson started to become dizzy, and soon his punches weren't connecting properly. He felt a tight grip on his tail, then his wrists. Something wrapped around his neck, choking him, and suddenly he was being lifted. His feet were trapped in the hands of red monsters, and he couldn't move at all.

*

'Hey! How *do* you kill a monster?' called out Jim with a big grin as Nelson was presented to him. 'Seriously, how is it done? I mean, do you just tear him to pieces? Chop off his head?'

Nelson tried to block Jim's words from his mind and focus on breaking free from the monsters' grasp.

'Anyone?' said Jim. 'Does anyone know the best way to kill him?'

Through the crowd of Jim's army pushed a chubby pink monster. When he had reached Jim's side he looked up at his master and licked his lips with a long grey tongue.

'I will eats him,' said the monster, and the army cheered at this fantastic idea.

'You can do that?' said Jim, sounding impressed.

'Mmm . . .' said the monster hungrily. 'He gonna burn in ma belly.'

'NO!' roared Nelson, struggling to escape.

'You can't fit all of him in at once, can you?' asked Jim of his greedy pink monster.

The monster nodded and opened its mouth, which seemed to dislocate at the jaw so that the bottom row of teeth fell almost to the ground.

'Wow! Impressive,' said Jim.

'PLEASE DON'T DO THIS!' roared Nelson, but Jim just shook his head and gestured for his monsters to proceed.

They suddenly rushed forward and crammed Nelson

into the pink monster's mouth, which slammed shut like an oven door.

Jim's monsters cheered and lifted their master high above their heads.

'REVENGE!' cried Jim triumphantly.

'REVENGE!' roared Jim's monster army.

LAST THOUGHTS

Nelson had been inside Nosh's belly many times before. Until now, it had been the most appalling place Nelson had ever been, but the belly of Jim's pink greedy monster was even worse. Firstly the smell, which was like hot vomit. Then there was what it felt like: there was a sweaty stickiness to the stomach walls, and at the bottom was a shallow pool of acid that was slowly eating away at Nelson's skin.

Nelson knew he was about to be incinerated. He could already feel the heat intensifying in the stomach walls. He could even hear the cheers of the monsters outside as they waited for the final blast of flames to erupt from the pink monster's head. These would be Nelson's last thoughts . . .

He didn't want to die. He wanted to live. More specifically, Nelson wanted to live as a normal boy and maybe even grow into an adult one day. But that was never going to happen now, and he just had to accept it. It was at this moment, one of the very last moments of his life, that Nelson's family appeared. Not literally – that would be impossible as there was barely enough room for

Nelson, let alone anyone else – but in his thoughts. The image of the photo that was taken at the party appeared to Nelson as clearly in his mind as if it were right in front of him. The sight of their faces, and the love that they felt for him, made his heart swell. Right there and then, Nelson Green realized that there was an even bigger reason to go on living than his own sense of self-preservation. The reason to go on was his family.

And with that thought, the pink monster who had eaten Nelson exploded into a thousand tiny pink pieces.

WHAT IN THE WORLD
JUST HAPPENED?

The thought of his family had not just made Nelson's heart swell, it had made his entire body swell. In fact, 'swell' doesn't really describe what happened accurately. It was more like Nelson had exploded from his original size to the size of a house, as quickly as a hot buttered kernel of corn pops into a puffy white cloud of popcorn.

Jim and his monsters were sent tumbling backwards in all directions as the massive and mighty Nelson Green stood towering over them, still dripping in stomach juice. He looked as if a four-year-old had had way too much sugar before designing their own Godzilla. For a moment Nelson didn't understand how he had survived or why the cathedral looked so small, but then it clicked. He was alive, and he was huge, and it was all because of the love he felt for his family.

What a day he was having.

Nelson looked down at Jim's little monsters scattering around his feet, and felt his lips pucker and protrude until they were sticking right out of his face like a trumpet.

'HOOOOOOOOOONK!'

The noise was so loud that all radio waves, TV signals and electricity within a three-mile radius were blacked out by the sonic shockwaves emanating from his giant lungs.

Jim's fear of what he was now facing was shared with his monsters. They knew their master was scared and they ran to attack the great Nelson. It was pathetic, really. Though Jim's monsters bit and punched and beat at Nelson's legs and feet, Nelson barely felt a thing. He knew a fight was a waste of time and that the best way to end this quickly was to do what they'd done.

And so with his four arms, and the hand at the end of his blue and rubbery tail, Nelson began picking up handfuls of monsters and shovelling them into his great trumpet-like mouth.

The taste? Well, as you can probably guess, it was hardly a delicious snack. It transpires that evil tastes worse than fried soiled nappies, but this was hardly the moment to complain about the cuisine.

Jim's bird monsters flew into the air and tried to peck at Nelson's head, but all Nelson had to do was swing his head from side to side for his horns to knock the bird monsters out of the air. A few of them escaped impact and dive-bombed Nelson's face. One of them became impaled on a giant cactus needle sticking out of Nelson's cheek. Nelson pulled the bird monster off like you would pull an olive from a cocktail stick, before swallowing the screaming bird monster whole. Yuck! That one tasted like earwax and public toilets. His great tongue, the size of a surfboard, licked his cheeks and collected up any remaining bird monsters still trying to attack his face. One of Jim's bird monsters had tried to attack Nelson by flying up his nose. Not a bad idea . . . but this only made Nelson sneeze. The bird monster shot out of his nostrils, contained within a huge gelatinous blob of green cactus juice that covered the floor.

'Waaaah! No! Nooo!' cried Jim, his head only just above the green goo while his body was trapped inside it.

Nelson bent down and with all four hands scooped up the goo.

'Please! Don't eat me!' cried Jim, but Nelson had no intention of eating him. With the rubbery blue hand at the end of his tail, Nelson plucked Jim out of the handful of goo like you would extract a hair from an otherwise lovely bowl of soup, dropped him on the ground, and then began to fill his mouth with great handfuls of goo-covered monsters.

Don't go thinking Nelson was enjoying this. He was finding this as disgusting as you are, but when you are trying to rid the world of a monster army you can't go getting squeamish. Anyway, the worst part wasn't eating the monsters; it was the wriggling and squirming Nelson could feel as they filled up his stomach.

Nelson burped, and a plume of purple gas rose from his nostrils. Something yellow caught his eye, and Nelson noticed the last of Jim's monsters: a bird monster on the rail of the Whispering Gallery. Nelson plucked it from the rail, dropped it into his mouth, and then bent low to address his enemy, who was cowering on the cathedral floor.

'I've done you a favour,' boomed the voice of the great Nelson.

Jim could not reply. He just shivered in fear.

'Trust me, living with monsters is harder than you think.' Nelson felt his stomach gurgle. Oh no. He was about to erupt.

Nelson crouched before the main door, which, even though it had been blown wide open by Jim's monsters, was still not big enough for him to walk through. He lay on his stomach, dragged himself through the doorway and stood up in the street, just in time to feel the flames shoot out of the top of his head. It looked like a rocket launching upside down, and the flames burned so fiercely that they pushed Nelson down and down, making him shorter and shorter. And they did not stop burning until Nelson was back to his normal size, though still very much a monster.

'Urgh,' said Nelson with a shudder, black smoke swirling around him. 'That was absolutely disgusting.'

Every single human being in the area surrounding St Paul's screamed and ran as fast as they could away from the immediate vicinity. They still could not see Nelson, but they saw the flames and the destruction, and no one wants to hang around and take selfies with something as frightening as that going on.

Back inside the cathedral, Jim collapsed on the floor. It was all over, and once again, he felt like the loser in life. He felt hopeless and angry, and tears sprang from his eyes.

Nelson walked back into the cathedral, black smoke still swirling from the pepper-pot holes on the top of his head. 'It's all right,' he said. 'It's over now.' He felt the clarity and certainty he used to feel when he was with his monsters. They may not have been in the building with him now, but somehow the clarity was still there, and it meant he knew exactly what to do next.

'How is it over?' sobbed Jim. He was so weak, confused and cold that his body began to shake. The craving to be back on the sin extractor was unbearable.

'Because we're not going to fight any more, and you're gonna make a new start for yourself.'

Jim snorted. He clearly found the idea of a new start preposterous.

'The thing is,' said Nelson, 'I don't know why I think this, but something tells me you're not really a bad person. You're just a bit of a mess, aren't you?'

Jim just shivered, his teeth chattering like castanets.

''S'all right, nobody's perfect, but everyone deserves a second chance,' said Nelson.

'Not me. I'm just gonna go to jail for the rest of my life.'

'Nah. There'll be police and ambulances and all that stuff arriving here in a minute, but you're going to be long gone.'

Nelson reached out to Jim with one of his red hands, and Jim flinched.

'I'm not going to hurt you,' said Nelson. 'In fact, I think you're gonna like this.' Nelson scooped a handful of green goo from Jim's shoulder and presented it to him as a gift.

'This is cactus juice. We call it the cactus cocktail. A bellyful of this will give you power you'd never believe.'

'I don't understand,' murmured Jim.

'It's like rocket fuel. It puts your body and your mind into, like, a super-mode. It also heals any health injuries and makes you think straight. Here.'

Nelson gestured for Jim to take the goo.

'Once you've swallowed it, you're gonna feel fantastic and see everything clearly. Like, really clearly. And that's when you are going to run away and start a new life. And it can be any life you want, anywhere you want.'

Jim tentatively took the goo from Nelson's hand, though much of it slid though his fingers.

'Don't worry,' said Nelson with a smile. 'It tastes better than it looks.'

Jim nodded sadly, opened his mouth, and swallowed the green cactus juice.

'Well?' said Nelson.

'It's a bit lemony,' said Jim.

'Now, in a few seconds you're going to feel amazing, but it won't last more than twenty-four hours, OK? Afterwards you'll need a massive sleep, but until then you are going to run as fast and as far away from here as you can – got that?'

Jim nodded, his cheeks already flushed with new energy.

'Ready?'

'I feel incredible,' said Jim with a gasp.

'And do you know where you're going?'

The cactus juice lit Jim's brain up like a Christmas tree, and all at once his thoughts became clear.

'Scotland. My dad lives there. I haven't seen him since my parents divorced. You see, I was always angry at him, but I think if I gave him a second chance . . .'

'Yeah, Jim, I don't need all the details – just get going,' urged Nelson.

'Wow. This stuff is amazing.'

'OK. On your marks, get set . . . GO!' said Nelson, and

Jim shot off out of the cathedral like a racehorse out of the starting gate.

'Woooo-hooo!' cried Jim as he reached a speed usually associated with Formula One racing.

THE SLEEPING PARTY

Though he looked like the very definition of a freak and his entire family were lying on the floor of the crypt, Nelson felt calm and clear headed. He could hear the sirens of the emergency service vehicles on their way to the scene and the shouts and cries of distress coming from the street outside.

The purple gas had gone, but everyone at the wedding was still fast asleep. Nelson touched his mother's head with one of his little orange arms and knew at once that the cut she had received to the top of her head would need nothing more than cleaning up and a bandage. His dad was covered in dust, and his arms were wrapped around his wife. It was the first time Nelson had noticed how perfectly they suited each other.

Yes, a lot of the guests were going to wake up and experience a great deal of shock, but they'd get over it. The most important thing to do, in the few seconds Nelson had left before the police arrived, was change.

The sin extractor was covered in a layer of dust, and two of the legs were bent, which made the table lean at an awkward angle.

With his powerful red hands, Nelson twisted the bent legs back into an upright position. There was a very loud snore and Nelson turned to see Rodeo Jones asleep on the stage with the microphone pressed up to his mouth, his snore hugely amplified.

Nelson chuckled, took a deep breath, and with trumpet-like lips blew every grain of dust from the sin extractor.

'HOOOOONK!'

Satisfied that it was clear and ready to use, Nelson bent down to look under the table. There were no copper test tubes, so the extractions were just going to pour on to the floor.

He took one last look around the room at the sleeping party guests and, feeling convinced that none of them would wake up in the next minute or so, he lowered himself backwards on to the needles.

The pain was like an electric shock. It made his eyes pop, his limbs stiffen like wood, and his mouth open in a silent scream.

And then the pain was gone, and Nelson was no longer lying on the sin extractor but riding on a cow through the Brazilian countryside, his monsters riding beside him on their own cows, racing towards a spectacular sunset as Abba's song 'SOS' played on a speaker in his backpack. The feeling was utterly thrilling, not just because he was leading a cow stampede, but because he was sharing the experience with his seven incredible friends.

'HA HA!' roared Nosh. 'We riding da cows, Nelly-son!'

While Nelson was submerged in this happy memory, the sin extractor worked its magic. The table shook as the seven monsters were drawn out of Nelson's soul and spilt like steaming hot oil on to the floor beneath. And as they hissed and squirmed and bubbled back to life, Nelson's body returned to its original shape, though completely naked.

WELCOME BACK

The chaos Jim Tindle and his ugly army had inflicted upon Pogo and Doody's wedding was nothing compared to the uproar that followed. Police, ambulances, nosey onlookers, TV news, and hysterical guests all shouting at once, now everyone was awake again.

They had found Nelson asleep outside in the garden. It was a pretty convincing act except for one thing: why was Nelson shoeless and wearing one of two matching bathrobes, both monogrammed, that Nelson's mother had had made as a wedding gift for Pogo and Doody? Nelson said he had spilt punch all over his clothes and had taken the gown as an emergency measure. his mum was very annoyed with Nelson for having ruined the surprise. Of course, Pogo and Doody were utterly delighted, and anyway, Nelson could hardly consider telling them the truth – that his real clothes were lying in shreds in a bin next to the bus stop.

'That man Jim has gone for good, hasn't he?' whispered Celeste when she was certain no one could hear them.

'Yes, it's all over. But never tell anyone who he was.'

'What happened?'

'Uh . . . Long story. But got some good news. My monsters are back.'

'They're here?'

'Not here. They'd be a nightmare to have around right now. I told them to meet us at Ivan's workshop in a few hours. They said to say hi.'

On the roof of the number 275 bus, seven monsters celebrated their return to life by howling and growling and crowing and laughing. Nosh, Stan, Miser, Hoot, Crush, Puff and Spike were back to their old selves. Even Stan was back to his original size. Fruit bats from London Zoo circled in the sky above and followed the bus all the way to the end of Ivan's road, where the monsters leaped off, on to the roof of the bus shelter.

'Ah, it's good to be back, lads,' said Stan, with all the satisfaction of a king having enjoyed a feast.

'It's just lucky we didn't kill Nelson,' moaned Spike as he slid down the side of the bus shelter and on to the pavement with the others.

'Lucky?' said Stan sounding offended. 'It wasn't luck that he survived. Nelson knew what he was doin'.'

'We didn't, though . . . did we?' said Puff sheepishly.

'I believe Nelson has forgiven us for turning him into an abomination,' hissed Miser. 'Now I think the matter is over and we can refrain from mentioning our mistake again.'

'Hear, hear!' cheered Hoot, and Crush skipped ahead of them all, honking all the way to Ivan's house.

'HONK! HONK! HOOOOONK!'

SCOTLAND

The rain was falling so hard on the roof of the little farmhouse that the farmer  didn't hear the doorbell ring. He didn't even hear the knocking on his door, and it wasn't until he went to draw the curtains for the night that he realized there was someone outside. At first he jumped with fright, but the face looking back at him in the rain smiled, and all at once the farmer's fright was gone, to be replaced by the warm feeling of seeing a face he loved.

'Jim,' said the farmer as he threw open the front door. 'Come in, son, come in.'

'Hello, Dad,' said Jim with a big smile on his face and tears in his eyes.

WHAT ARE WE GOING TO DO ABOUT YOUR MONSTERS?

With their home destroyed and in need of huge amounts of repair work, the Green family's options were simple. They could either use the insurance money to rent a nice house while theirs was being repaired, or rent a smaller, not-so-nice apartment and use the money left over to go on holiday. And of course, that is what they all chose to do.

It was actually Uncle Pogo's idea, and everyone agreed it was a brilliant solution to a dreadful situation. While the builders took care of fixing up the wreck that was their house, and Minty stayed next door with George (but refused to engage with him unless she was being fed), the Greens were going to spend three weeks in Greece. It would take longer than that to repair the damage at home, but at least they could put it all behind them for a while and enjoy a little sunshine.

The biggest problem for Nelson wasn't that half his house was missing; it was that he still had to work out how to undo the curse that meant he wasn't growing. The day before they were due to go on holiday, Nelson called a meeting at Ivan's workshop, where, together with

Celeste, Nelson and his monsters plotted their next move. To be honest, it was hours of them all talking absolute nonsense, so I will just skip to the part where they began to make progress.

'They can't be reabsorbed . . .' said Celeste, who paced the floor like a detective piecing together a crime.

'We all know that!' roared Stan.

'Let her finish!' hissed Nelson. 'God, you lot are doing my head in. Carry on, Cel.'

'And you don't want them to die?' she continued.

'Obviously, it would be great to avoid that.' Crush hugged Nelson's leg and honked his appreciation.

Is there anywhere they could go that would be far enough away to break the link between you all? signed Ivan.

'It doesn't matter where they go – we'll always be connected.'

'Unless . . .' hissed Miser.

'Unless what, Miser?'

'Unless we go somewhere that is not connected in time.'

'The Bang Stone. We could be disconnected by time,' said Nelson, and Miser nodded.

The monsters fell silent. They all knew this was the answer. They could break their connection with Nelson and stay alive by living in a different time. The only question was, where and when in time should they go?

Ivan handed Nelson and Celeste a mug of tea each and sat on the edge of the workbench. Nelson took a chocolate biscuit from a plate, and his monsters all did the same. Ivan couldn't help but laugh at the sight of all those biscuits disappearing into thin air.

BOMBS AWAY!

To use Nelson's father's expression, 'The flight to Athens is leaving at an ungodly hour.' By 'ungodly', he meant 5 a.m., which meant they all had to be at the airport at 3 a.m., which meant leaving home at 2 a.m., which meant setting an alarm to wake them up at 1 a.m. Ungodly indeed. But once they were on their way, it was a wonderful journey.

Nelson insisted on a window seat so he could watch his monsters climb aboard the luggage hold beneath the plane.

'Who are you waving to?' asked Nelson's mum, who was peering at him over her inflight magazine.

'Oh, just a bloke working down there on the runway,' lied Nelson, and he turned back to see Stan hurl Crush up on to the conveyor belt carrying luggage into the hold.

Ivan was sitting directly in front of Nelson and turned to look at him through the gap between the seat and the wall of the plane.

Are they on board? signed Ivan.

Yes, signed Nelson, and Ivan grinned and winked before turning back.

Everyone in Nelson's family was asleep before the

plane took off, which was no surprise, given how early they had risen. Only Nelson remained wide awake as the plane turned at the end of the runway ready for take-off.

TAP! TAP! TAP!

Nelson's mother stirred from her sleep but thankfully was not woken by the sound of Hoot tapping on Nelson's window. Nelson sighed at the sight of his beloved yellow friend. It was clear he had been tricked by the other monsters yet again.

'I say! Dear boy! I seem to have been locked out of the plane!'

Nelson threw up his hands in an expression that said, 'What do you want me to do about it?'

'MAYBE YOU COULD OPEN THE DOOR AND LET ME IN?'

Nelson shook his head at this absurd idea. The plane began to accelerate down the runway.

'AH! I SEE! IN THAT CASE I SHALL HAVE TO FLY ALONGSIDE!'

Nelson nodded.

'VERY WELL! BYE-BYE FOR NOW!' cried Hoot, and he let go of the plane as it took off. The engines roared, but Nelson could have sworn he heard raucous monster laughter coming from below.

The minibus that took them all from Athens airport was perfect. Not only could they all fit comfortably inside with their luggage, but the roof was big enough to hold the monsters, who sang all the way to the seaport. Here they boarded a huge ferry that would take them to the island of Syros. After leaving their luggage by the great ferry doors, the family headed upstairs, where they found a cafe selling coffee and cheese-filled pastries.

To Nelson's delight, the outside deck was vast, and there was plenty of room to sit with his monsters without drawing attention to himself or them.

HONK! went the ferry as it left the port.

'HONK!' said Crush in reply, and the monsters laughed their heads off.

The blue skies, the sea breeze and the dazzling sunshine did wonders for everyone's spirits, and by the time the clusters of white houses on the island of Syros were in view, they already felt like they'd been on holiday for a week.

Pogo and Doody had stayed on the island of Syros together during the recording of their TV series. It was here they had discovered the shipwreck containing the monstrous results of Master Buzzard's experiment with the sin extractor. They had also made friends with some of the locals, who were delighted to welcome them back and had helped them find a cheap house to rent in a little fishing harbour. The house was like every other house on the island: white and smooth and square. In any other part of the world these houses might look peculiar, like quirky, stone butter dishes, but here on the island of

Syros they looked like the only kind of house you would ever need.

It was without doubt the best holiday Nelson had ever had. Even though his monsters could not live with them in the house (without causing chaos), they loved staying in the fishing boats that were anchored at night, and during the day they could choose from any number of little beaches to play on. Some of the beaches were so small you could only fit a dozen people on them, and many of these you couldn't get to unless you climbed around the rocks.

And one of the beaches, a tiny cove just a few minutes' walk from their house, was exactly like the dream Nelson and his monsters had shared during their super-sleep. The water was just right. Not only was it clear and shallow so that you could wade out and splash about playing Frisbee, but it was just the right temperature – cool enough to give you relief from the sun, but warm enough that you could play in it all day.

'BOMBS AWAY!' cried Stan and Nelson as they both jumped off a high rock into the sea. They crashed into the water, a billion bubbles whirling around them, and through his goggles Nelson could see Miser walking around on the ocean floor as if he were walking down an ordinary street. His long rubber arms sifted through the stones and shells to find the loveliest and most precious ones, but instead of keeping them to himself, he had brought them back to the beach and presented them to Celeste.

Hoot stood on a rock with a seagull called Carlos.

'So you know Edna, do you?' said Hoot.

'Oh yes, everyone knows Edna,' said Carlos.

'Lovely gal – or gull I should say, ha ha! But do you ever find her a bit, you know, prone to exaggerate?'

'Edna does enjoy being the centre of attention.'

'Yes she does! Carlos, you've got her spot on.'

As Hoot and Carlos chatted, Nosh's head erupted in a short blast of flames. Flotsam and jetsam turned out to be Nosh's favourite snack of all time. Yes, even better than mangoes. He would sit in the shallow water and collect bits of seaweed and old soft wood until he had a great pile to eat. It was the saltiness he loved the most, so it didn't really matter if he was eating a branch from a tree or a lost flip-flop. Between snacks, Nosh licked the stones and shells, and enjoyed the feeling of being weightless as he bobbed about in the water like a pink balloon.

Celeste and Ivan were snorkelling around the reef where Crush was splashing about in the rock pools and making friends with the little crabs.

191

The only downside of being by the sea was all the attention Nelson was getting from the fish, and having jumped off the rock into the sea, the fish in the area quickly assembled around him and carried him swiftly back to shore.

'Wait! I want to stay in the sea! I don't want to get out!' spluttered Nelson as he lifted his head from the sand, but it was impossible to tell them not to do this and it made Stan laugh his head off.

Puff, as you can imagine, did nothing but sleep. Nelson had made him a hammock by stringing a large beach towel between two thin trees, and the sea breeze rocked Puff back and forth all day long.

The only one who never seemed to be enjoying it as much as the others was Spike. He was either too hot in the sun or too cold in the sea, and when they tried to get him to join in with a game, he was too tired, and when they let him sit it out, he complained of being bored.

'He's never satisfied, so whatcha gonna do?' said Stan. Nelson didn't like seeing one of his monsters in a bad mood, but Stan was right: some people are only happy being unhappy.

It was at yet another ungodly hour that Nelson was woken in his bunk-bed by Crush nuzzling him. It took him a few seconds to remember where he was and to notice that the monsters had gathered beside his bed.

'What are you doing here? You're supposed to hide out

on one of the boats,' whispered Nelson. Ivan was asleep in the bunk below and Nelson could hear him snoring gently.

'It's time to go,' said Spike.

'Go where? Where are we going?'

'Not you. Us. It's time for us to go,' said Spike, who smiled for the first time in his life.

Crush could see Nelson was hurt by the realization of what Spike meant, and nuzzled deeper into Nelson's chest.

'Why do you want to go now? It's the middle of the night. The holiday's not over for another two weeks.'

None of the monsters replied. They simply stood still, looking up at Nelson in the moonlight.

Nelson pulled on his shorts, T-shirt and sandals, and retrieved the plastic pot containing the Bang Stone from under his bed. He opened the lid, and although the stone was still contained within a small ceramic pot, the scent of sulphur filled the room. Ivan stirred and turned over in his sleep.

'Shh. Let's go,' said Stan.

The dusty road leading from the house down to the harbour was bright white in the moonlight. The gentle crunch of Nelson and his seven monsters walking on the gravel, and the distant sound of waves lapping the shore, could not have been more peaceful.

'But why leave now?' said Nelson again, once they

were far enough away from the house not to be heard.

'We're just . . . delaying . . . the inevitable, Nelson,' said Puff.

'Yeah,' agreed Stan, and he pointed up at the moon. 'Besides, it's a perfect night for it.'

'Yup, me don't wanna leave Nelly-son, but it's time to go,' said Nosh, sounding far more grown up than usual.

'But how will I know if it's worked?'

'If we succeed in breaking the connection, you will most certainly feel it, as will we,' said Miser.

'Oh, so you mean it's going to hurt,' said Nelson, and Miser nodded.

'Well, here we are, my dears,' said Hoot, coming to a stop at the end of a long wooden jetty with lots of little fishing boats tied to it. No one explained why this was to be the place they said goodbye; they simply felt like it was the right place, and that was enough.

Nelson looked down at his little monsters, and in that moment he thought his heart would break in two.

'Oh, we feel the same,' said Spike clutching his chest. 'But the worst part will be over soon.'

'I don't want it to be over,' said Nelson, his voice trembling as he tried to stop the tears rushing out of his eyes. Crush ran forward and leaped up into Nelson's arms.

'It's been a pleasure, Nelson,' said Stan, trying to look tough but failing to hide his tears.

'Yeah, it has, hasn't it?' Nelson was crying openly now. There was no point trying to stop it.

'Me loves ya, Nelly-son,' Nosh said as he hugged Nelson's legs.

'Careful, Nosh! You're gonna knock me into the sea.' The monsters were relieved to find something to laugh at.

'Bye, Nelson,' said Puff with a big smile and wide-open eyes that reflected the full moon above them.

'Puff, I am going to miss you so much. And Hoot . . .' Nelson trailed off as he hugged his big yellow bird-like monster.

'Goodbye, dear friend,' Hoot whispered into Nelson's ear. 'May you live a long and happy life.'

Hearing this, Nelson could not help but begin to sob again. Crush squeezed tighter into Nelson's neck.

'Hooooonk,' cooed Crush, and Nelson felt a wave of happiness fight back the tide of sadness threatening to engulf him.

'Master Nelson, please remember we are made from you and therefore still a part of you,' said Miser as he opened the ceramic jar containing the Bang Stone.

'I know, I know,' muttered Nelson breathlessly.

'I don't understand that at all,' sobbed Hoot.

'Never mind, let's just do this,' urged Stan.

Crush let go of Nelson and slid down on to the deck. The other monsters gathered around him, and Miser passed Nosh the Bang Stone.

'Are you sure you know where you're going?' Once again Nelson realized he sounded just like his mother.

'Oh yeah, we know where and when we're going,' said Stan with a chuckle.

'Where? What year?' said Nelson. Spike took hold of Nelson's hand.

'We decided it's better you don't know, or you'll be thinking about it all the time. And you have to start moving on now, Nelson.'

'But don't worry, dear boy,' said Hoot with a wink. 'We'll be absolutely fine.'

'Better stand back, Nelson, you know what these things are like,' warned Spike.

'HONK! HONK! HONK!' said Crush, and it sounded so rude and funny that Nelson laughed.

And as he laughed, Nosh popped the Bang Stone into his mouth, the monsters clustered around him and . . . *BANG!* They were gone in a puff of blue smoke.

GROWING PAINS

The pain was instant and awful. Nelson collapsed on to the wooden jetty, the end of which had been broken in the blast. He clutched the sides of his head, which pounded as if someone were squeezing him in a vice, while his back, knees and ankles felt as if they were being taken apart bit by bit. Nelson screamed, but his face was buried into his balled fists and no one was close enough to hear him. The tips of his fingers pulsed with pain, and as he opened his eyes he saw his fingernails growing and stretching. At the very same time, Nelson could feel his hair getting longer, being dragged out of his skull, strand by strand, until he could see it hanging in front of his eyes.

Though the pain consumed him, Nelson knew what was happening: now that the monsters had gone, the curse had been lifted, and all the growing he would have done over the last year was happening in just a few seconds.

The fish in the harbour could only gaze up at Nelson, who lay breathless on the wooden jetty. If they could have leaped out of the water and stroked the hair from his eyes, they would have done. Instead, they swam away, back into the cool, moonlit waters and hoped he would feel better soon.

The sun was about to rise when Nelson staggered back to the little house like someone who had just completed a marathon. The hardest part of the journey was getting back up the steps into his bunk-bed because his knees were as creaky and stubborn as cellar doors, but once his body had flopped on to the mattress and the breeze from the ceiling fan touched the back of his neck, Nelson fell into a deep and dream-filled sleep.

When he finally awoke, the day had passed, the sun was already setting, and he found Celeste sitting on the end of his bed.

'You've changed.'

'What?'

'Your hair and everything. Even the little freckle on the end of your nose is back.'

'Is it?'

'Yeah. They've gone, haven't they?'

Nelson burst into tears, and Celeste hugged him.

'You'll be all right. Want me to give you a haircut?'

'Do I need one?'

'Yep.'

Celeste had been careful to wake Nelson while their parents were out enjoying a dinner at a local Greek tavern with Ivan and some of the locals in town. His mother had put Nelson's sleepiness down to being exhausted from the heat and swimming, and had enjoyed a few too many gin and tonics to notice the change in Nelson's hair when she came in to check on him.

'Sit here, I'll be right back,' said Celeste. She had put a stool from the kitchen right at the end of the garden, overlooking the sea. The moon was bright, and the view of the harbour was so beautiful it was hard to imagine there could be anywhere else in the universe as perfect as this. The garden suddenly lit up with fairy lights, and Celeste called from inside, 'Did the lights just go on?!'

'YES!' replied Nelson.

Celeste reappeared carrying a comb, scissors and water spray.

'What'll it be, Nelson Green? Short back and sides?'

'Yes please.'

Celeste set to work, first spraying Nelson's hair with water, then combing it through and beginning to snip away.

'You know what I think? I think your monsters prove a point.'

'What point?'

'That we all have our bad sides, but we can use them for good. You know, like pride, anger, laziness, envy . . . all that stuff is technically bad, right? They were supposedly seven deadly sins, but they could do just as much good as bad. It's what you do with them that counts.'

Nelson puffed the wet hair off his nose and smiled, happy to be the brother of the best sister in the world.

IT TAKES TWO

Everyone cried at the party, even the priest who had married Doody and Pogo months ago, though that might have been because she had a terrible case of wind after drinking a bottle of fizzy water and eating an entire bowl of corn chips. It had been just over three weeks since they returned from the holiday, but Doody and Pogo were still determined to have their wedding party. The emotions of their guests were running as freely as the wine and food, and this meant that when Pogo and Doody began their first dance, the place erupted with cheers and whistles.

At first it had been a slow number – a melancholy song called 'Nature Boy' by Nat King Cole that Pogo and Doody swayed to. Nelson's mother tried to drag his father on to the dance floor, but he managed to stand his ground by pretending his back hurt.

Nelson felt a hand gently land on his shoulder and turned to find Ivan smiling at him.

You OK? he signed.

Nelson nodded and smiled.

They wanted me to give you this when the time was right. Ivan pulled an envelope out of his jacket pocket.

Nelson's heart raced. A present from his monsters? What on earth could be more fantastic than that?

What does it say?

You tell me.

Nelson tore the envelope open and there, in the worst handwriting he had ever seen, was the following note:

Dear Nelson,
We left you a present buried in your garden where we used to put the tent. Only use it in emergencies.
Love,
THE DEADLY SEVEN

Nelson guessed it must be cactus juice, and grinned from ear to ear at the thought of his monsters taking the time and care to leave him a present.

It hadn't been more than a verse or two before Nat King Cole suddenly stopped and was replaced by the intro to 'It Takes Two' by Rob Base and DJ E-Z Rock. Pogo and Doody threw off their jackets and faced each other like matadors. The lights went out and a laser struck the glitter ball hanging from the ceiling, sending beams of light in every direction. The wedding guests lost their minds as the beat kicked in and the two of them began to dance like they were in their own music video.

'OH MY GOD! THEY'RE DOING A ROUTINE!' screamed Nelson's mum.

Doody and Pogo were phenomenal. Their timing and their footwork were perfect, and the fact that Uncle Pogo had a false leg meant it was doubly impressive.

Nelson looked around at all the guests cheering and clapping for his uncles. There were Ivan and Celeste, leaping up and down as if they were in the mosh pit of a rock concert. Beside them were his parents and the team who had made Doody and Pogo's TV show, all of them swaying all over the place, having had way too much to drink. Bouncing up and down on the spot next to them, as if he were still on his trampoline, was his neighbour, George. Ever since the incident with Jim Tindle and his army of monsters, George had become much more chatty, and Nelson had taken his sister's advice to invite him along to the party.

Doody and Pogo hadn't finished their routine, but they threw their arms open wide and beckoned to all the guests to join them on the dance floor. No one could resist them. Nelson's mother grabbed Ivan and off they went. Celeste took George by the hand, and though George resisted at first, she succeeded in teasing him out of his comfort zone. Uncle Pogo crossed the room to ask Doody's auntie Ailsa, his only living relative, if she would like to dance, and though the lady was almost a hundred years old, she took hold of Pogo's hand and followed him on to the dance floor. Nelson's dad was dancing with Doody, and Nelson was genuinely shocked at how well his dad could dance.

Nelson didn't need a dance partner or an excuse to join in. He shimmied his way into the middle of the dancing crowd and lost himself in the music and the happiness of the moment.

GOODNIGHT, NELSON GREEN

It was way past midnight when Nelson climbed into the bed of his recently restored home and pulled the covers up to his chin. He had snuck into the garden as soon as the taxi had dropped them off, and while his parents went through their usual bathroom routines and loudly recounted their favourite parts of the day, Nelson dug up the bottle of cactus juice his monsters had left for him. It was full, but Nelson didn't open it. They had said it was for emergencies only, and that was what he would save it for.

Nelson's new bedroom was very cool. Now he had a bunk-bed under which sat a neat little desk and a little music system. His copy of the script of *Bugsy Malone* lay open on the desk, though he had learned every word of it and was ready for the first show next week. He loved being in the show, and he especially loved the splurge guns. It made him feel like a cooler version of himself. Katy Newman had cast herself as Blousey Brown, which meant they had to kiss each other briefly on stage. He was surprised to find he actually liked kissing her. His monsters would have been appalled to hear this and would certainly have made fun of him. Maybe there were a few upsides to not having them around.

The coolest thing about his new room was that his mother had allowed Nelson to paint on the wall next to his window, and as he had never been able to take a photo of his monsters, he had painted them instead. It was a colourful picture, and Nelson only needed to glance at it

for a smile to appear instantly on his face. He thought about his friends and where they might be. Were they happy? Were they safe? Was there enough to eat? Did they get as sad as he did at times?

As Nelson lay there feeling a little sadness begin to creep up on him, the bedroom door creaked open . . .

It was Minty.

Nelson had never seen the dog awake at night, let alone venture upstairs. She was clearly a little exhausted from climbing the stairs, but she continued to plod across Nelson's bedroom carpet and stopped beside his bed.

'Minty? What are you doing here?' said Nelson. As if in reply, the dog put its paw on Nelson's bed.

'What is it? You want to come up?'

At the sound of these words, Minty began to pant enthusiastically.

'I'll take that as a yes, then,' said Nelson, and he lifted Minty on to his bed.

No sooner had he done this than Minty curled up on top of Nelson's feet and went to sleep.

Nelson felt his sadness drift away, and a happy and sleepy feeling washed over him. Minty, who had never shown the slightest interest in anything much, had picked up on how Nelson was feeling and was here to comfort him. Finally, after all these years, Minty had decided to join the family.

As Minty snored, Nelson looked at the painting of his

monsters on the wall. He felt certain that wherever they were right now, they were safe and they were happy, and that everything was going to be fine.

And he was absolutely right.

THANK YOU . . .

. . . to Rachel Petty for being the most ingenious and supportive book editor I could hope to collaborate with.

To Sarah Hughes for taking over editing duties with such grace while Rachel was off having twins. To Rob Biddulph for his brilliant series of book covers. I love them, Rob. To Kat and Jo in marketing and publicity at Macmillan Children's Books for helping spread the word despite having to work with an author who is never around when you need him. To Rachel Vale and Tracey Ridgewell in the design department, and to everyone else at Macmillan Children's Books for making me feel so welcome.

To Felicity Rubinstein at Luytens & Rubinstein for her beautiful handmade coffee cups, the gossipy lunches and for letting me raid her book shop when I am lucky enough to visit. To Frank Wuliger at Gersh for the wise words, for being the only film agent in Hollywood to wear a fedora and for helping me up when 'the wheels fell off.'

To Hope Buxton, Jago Kubaisi, Flo Roberts, Nancy Stirling and all you wonderful readers who sent me cards and drawings of Nelson and his monsters. They all mean the world to me.

To my mum and dad for being the most loyal and loving fan club anyone could wish for. To my sons Oscar, Leo, Caspar and Asa for being the loveliest twits I have ever met and the inspiration for so many bad jokes and peculiar ideas. They were all for you and I hope you like them.

And finally to my magical best friend and co-pilot, Woz for . . . well, just everything. X